THE WHISKEY TRADERS

THE WHISKEY TRADERS

Wade Everett

GUNSMOKE

This hardback edition 2009
by BBC Audiobooks Ltd
by arrangement with
Golden West Literary Agency

ISBN 978 1 405 68236 7

British Library Cataloguing in Publication Data available.

Printed and bound in Great Britain by
CPI Antony Rowe, Chippenham, Wiltshire

1

FORT BENTON'S streets were a morass of mud from yesterday's hard rain. It had tapered off during the night, but the drizzle had continued all day. Brent Bargen shivered. The drizzle had soaked him through; a Montana May rain was usually a cold one. The rain was a cattleman's delight, but Brent cursed it. It had cost him a day's work yesterday and a soaking today, for a woodchopper couldn't afford the loss of two days' pay in a week. One day's loss wiped out the tiny margin he earned above the necessities; two days' loss and he buckled his belt tight enough to flatten his belly against his backbone.

His moccasins swished uncomfortably as he walked, and the chill that started in his feet was crawling up his legs. He needed a change into dry clothing and footwear, and he had neither. His boots had worn out last week, and the cost of a new pair was beyond him. Moccasins were cheap, but he hated to wear them. They were the delineation; they separated white man from Indian. Some white men still wore them. But they were secure in the knowledge their blood was untainted. They could wear anything they wanted.

Behind him, at the wharves, a steamboat whistled mournfully as its crew prepared to cast off the mooring lines. A crowd had gathered to watch its departure, but Brent didn't turn his head. He had seen all he wanted of steamboats. It should have an easier trip downriver. The rain had broken a dry spell and would raise the river, affording a deeper channel. The pilot could ease off some of his tension, for higher water would cover the sandbars.

Brent thought enviously of a pilot's job. It was a secure, well-paying one. But like a long list of jobs, it was out of his reach. He blamed one reason only, overlooking the lack of schooling and experience. The moment the fact of his Indian blood was known, nobody wanted him.

Everybody in steamboating made money—except the stevedores and woodchoppers. He could pick from those two

5

jobs. He had chosen woodchopping, not liking the thought of being burdened like some dumb animal.

The steamboat had brought up a huge cargo of raw alcohol from St. Louis. The raw spirits were consigned to the whiskey traders, and they would bring a truly handsome profit after being cut. But he would never see any of those profits. He belonged to the wrong class.

His hand closed on the coins in his pocket. That boat would be carrying his sweat, represented by the wood he had chopped for its fuel. A steamer's boilers were voracious, and it took a mountain of cordwood to satisfy them. A wood-chopper never had more than coins in his pocket, for he was never paid in proportion to the amount of work he did. It was a dull, racking existence, and a man's physical endurance couldn't be stretched enough to let him earn more than a pittance. But it was one of the few jobs open to a breed. He never avoided the term.

He could save the coins by going back to his miserable hovel, making his supper out of a can of beans, then crawling between his blankets. His eyes flashed rebellion. A man was entitled to more than that. He had carefully counted his coins, and they could be stretched to cover a drink and supper. For a few moments he would be warm; he could create a small escape, even though the illusion would be soon gone.

Nobody hailed him as he moved down the wooden walk. He knew many of the men he passed, but outside of a rare nod, there was no sign of recognition. He wanted it that way. Long ago he had learned that a loosening of his guard by putting trust in another man brought only hurt and humiliation. So now he lived in solitude as much as he could, deliberately smothering normal human impulse. The blood of two races conditioned him that way. He had too much white blood to think of accepting the Indian way of life, and because of his Indian blood the whites wouldn't accept him. It left him a lonely island, lashed and soured by rejection. It left him with no anchor, no foothold, and worst of all, no purpose. He had thought of drifting on to another country, but he knew he would find things no different there. Man drew his own little tight society about him and fought any attempt to penetrate it. A close observer could see a dozen examples of it here before he covered six blocks.

Fort Benton was an important town as a terminus for the river shipping. Its fur trade and traffic with the gold camps were diminishing, but enough new activities were building so that the loss of the first two was scarcely noticed. It was a wild town, and visitors were warned, "Walk in the middle of the street and mind your own business." The advice contained little jest.

Its streets were always crowded. Part of the original stockade and blockhouses still stood, though the town had spread beyond the earlier confines of its walls. The fur trappers had thinned out, and in their place were the wolfers, who lived by skinning wolves. No tougher breed of man walked. They led a lonely, dangerous life and were disliked by everyone. Even in town they stayed with their own, and their sole purpose here seemed to be to see how drunk they could get. Nobody tried to upset the arrangement, for the wolfers were a surly lot with hair-trigger tempers.

The whiskey traders were a relatively new class, and the profits from their illicit trade gave them their own special arrogance. Some people said that their financing came from some of the biggest names in Montana. None of it touched Brent, and he didn't bother to speculate on it.

The outlaws and horse thieves made another tight group, breaking the monotony of their lonely lives by occasional visits to Fort Benton. Their faces never relaxed, and their wary eyes weighed every happening. At the slightest alarm they disappeared into the breaks.

Brent knew the Missouri breaks well. It was a wild, almost inaccessible land. The law was totally ineffective for reaching into the breaks. Even the army gave it a wide berth, claiming prior attention to other matters. Brent didn't blame the law for not going into that rough land. Fifty lawmen could stumble around in it, every move watched by human eyes, and they would never see a man.

It was an immense, broken land, its cliffs sudden and precipitous. A few trails through it were rough and hard to find. The breaks held no towns and few houses, except for the skillfully hidden shacks of the outlaws. For all intents and purposes it was a forgotten land, and neither authority nor wanted man wanted it changed. It was covered with scrub pine, spruce, and cedar, scattered in the purple-shadowed coulees and on the hills that sprang up suddenly from vast canyon floors. It was a land of strange, wild beauty, but because of its human occupants, a land to be avoided.

A burly army sergeant swaggered down the street and brushed Brent hard. Brent sent a following glare after the man, and the sergeant was unaware of it. The troopers were another unpopular class, holding themselves above and apart from other life in the town. They drank hard and played hard, and the law rarely stepped in because of any of their offenses. The army authorities said crisply, they would punish their own, though Brent doubted it ever happened. The army, too, had its own peculiar brand of arrogance, matched only by that of the cattlemen. The cattlemen and army had an intense dislike for each other, and Brent had seen some noteworthy brawls. Fort Benton was a melting pot, a pot that simmered over frequently into senseless violence.

He heard the sodden plopping of hoofs in the muddy street behind him and whipped his head around. The sound of running hoofs in town always carried a note of emergency in it.

A dozen horsemen crowded the street, their mouths stretched wide with their yelling. Foot traffic halted, then broke for shelter. These were Broken Bit riders, and nobody crossed them. Usually, their forays into town consisted of yelling, firing a few random shots, and copious drinking. But they weren't averse to putting a bullet close enough to a man to see him dive from his feet. Sheriff Jess Haymes never stopped nor checked their fun, claiming it was only a harmless easing of spirits. Broken Bit brought a lot of business into town, and that was always the first consideration. Brent's blood heated whenever he saw them. They were the new lords of this land, and he suspected their dominion would grow. He had a personal quarrel with cattlemen. He had worked for three different outfits, and while his work had been satisfactory, the hands had roughed him into a fight. He was the one who was always fired, and he blamed his Indian blood for that.

Brent stood his ground, his face stony. They were shooting

8

now as they came, and he expected that. So far it was harmless shooting aimed at the sky, but the man nearest Brent dove from his feet, ending up in the muddy street.

That and the others ducking for cover was bad, for it attracted attention to Brent standing alone. The pinch-faced rider on the inside spotted him. He swung his pistol down, and a bullet gouged splinters at Brent's foot. It had to be a lucky shot, for nobody aimed that well from the back of a galloping horse. But another shot was coming. Brent could see it in the rider's face. He couldn't risk the next shot hitting him, and he dove for a place beside the man already in the mud.

He raised a mud-smeared, wrathful face and yelled after the rider, "You son-of-a-bitch."

The rider was half slewed around in his saddle, looking back at him. Brent didn't know whether or not the man had heard him, and he didn't care.

He stood as Broken Bit whipped around the far corner. He used the edge of his palm to scrape mud from himself, and he was boiling. The other man also stood. He glanced at his muddy clothes and swore before he looked at Brent. "That wasn't wise."

Brent glared at him. "What wasn't wise?"

"Yelling at him like that. He may have heard you. All right, all right," he said hastily as he caught Brent's expression. "It's your affair."

Brent's eyes smoldered as he watched him move away. He felt no appreciation of the warning. What was he supposed to do—just stand here and take something like that?

A wry sense of humor returned to him. That was exactly what he had done—except that he had lain in the mud instead of standing. He ran his hand over his face, getting most of the mud off it. He could do nothing more for his clothes, and it mattered little. The mud couldn't make him any colder than he was.

Brent moved toward the nearest saloon, needing that drink more than ever. For several feet to the right and left of the doors he couldn't see the walk for the discarded playing cards. Every saloon followed the policy of throwing old cards out of the door.

He paused just inside the swinging doors, feeling the appreciable increase of warmth. His face was harsh hewn as a granite knob, the cheekbones high and prominent over hollowed cheeks. The nose was thin and predatory over an angry slit of a mouth. The face and coarse black hair bespoke the Indian blood in him, and the blue eyes were a startling surprise. He could thank a father he had never seen for them. He stood a fraction under six feet, his body as lean and durable as a rawhide thong. Its leanness was deceptive, for he had the muscular torso of the horseman on thin horseman's legs.

He was relieved that the place was almost empty. He would have his warming drink, then cross the street for supper.

One man at the bar turned to watch Brent's progress to its end. He was a big man with huge hands that looked clumsy. He wore a deputy's star on his vest, and his heavy glance was slow and thoughtful. Brent knew his name—Lucas Moore —though he had never exchanged a word with the man. He wanted no contact with the law, for any brush with it would automatically go against him. The man had been here six months, and Brent felt contempt for anybody who would take Haymes' orders.

He ordered his drink, and the bartender pointedly didn't pour until Brent paid for it. Brent's resentment showed in his eyes, but he was careful not to push against the bartender's attitude. The bartender could act as he pleased; he had the law here to back him up.

He took the drink in sips, wanting to make its warming last as long as he could. He heard the clatter of many boots at the door and watched in the back mirror. His face stiffened. He had picked the wrong saloon. Broken Bit was pouring into the place.

He took the remaining whiskey in a gulp and set his glass down. He would wait until they were engrossed in their drinking, then try to slip out unnoticed.

He wasn't that lucky. The pinch-faced rider spotted him and changed his course to come directly to him.

Brent watched him in the mirror. The man was husky enough through the chest and shoulders, and those bandy legs gave him a rolling gait. His face had seen a lot of rugged wear. A scar bisected one cheek from eye to mouth, and

Brent saw evidence of other misadventures in that face. He would say the man was a brawler and enjoyed it.

He stopped behind Brent and pushed a lock of sandy hair out of his eyes. "Ain't you the one who yelled something at me?"

Brent's mouth tightened. He kept his eyes on the bar mirror. The rest of them pressed closer, their eyes bright with a savage expectancy.

"Goddam it. You look at me when I'm talking to you. And you answer me. What did you yell at me?"

"Make him talk to you, Sandy," one of the riders said. "Or maybe you ain't big enough."

Brent learned that a man's soul could rave and crawl at the same time. They wouldn't let it stop here. They would egg Sandy on until it broke into open violence. He couldn't fight them all. He wanted to. God, how he wanted to. But if he kept his head, he might be able to get away without the moment worsening. You mean run, don't you, his outraged soul raved at him.

He turned slowly and didn't dare let Sandy see his eyes. They contained too much hating. "I didn't yell anything."

Sandy was the center of attention, and he enjoyed it. "You calling me a liar? You damned—" He searched for the term he wanted and found it: "breed. We don't let no damned breed talk to a white man that way." Sandy advanced a menacing step. "What did you yell at me? Or do I have to tear it out of you?"

The rage and sick despair made a sour mixture in Brent's throat. He wasn't going to be able to escape anything. This was amusement to Sandy, and the man wasn't going to pass it up.

He doubted he could get in more than one blow before they swarmed him under. But he could make it a good one; he could try to tear off Sandy's face with it.

"Damn you." He moved before surprise could set on Sandy's face. He got the leverage of a shoulder behind his fist, and he felt lips pulp and teeth break under the blow. He knocked Sandy back into the men behind him, and it came too quickly for them to be set for it.

They let Sandy slide to the floor, and he sat there, a dazed disbelief on his face. He shook his head to clear it. He bled

11

at the mouth and nose, and he raised a hand to his face, further smearing the blood on it. The confusion on his face slowly cleared. "Why goddam you."

The faces ringing Brent in were stone hard. He had kicked over the cart for sure now, and there was no escaping what would follow. "It looks like we've got to knock a little respect into him, Sandy," one of them drawled.

Sandy tried to get to his feet, but his muscles weren't up to it yet. He swore viciously. "Save a little for me."

They came at him in a rush, and it was impossible to guard against all the flying fists. They slammed at him from every direction, and in a few seconds he was dazed and bleeding. His senses were scattering, and his blows were blind and unaimed. He wished he had a gun or a knife; he wished he had any kind of a weapon.

"Hold it!" he heard a voice yell. It seemed to come from a tremendous distance.

Moore shoved men aside to get to Brent. He swung those slate-gray eyes from face to face. "Damn it, Lucas," one of them argued, "if you think we're going to let that breed get away with this—"

Brent leaned against the bar, needing its support. His face hurt, and he could feel blood dripping from a couple of cuts. He was grateful to Moore. The man had saved him from a worse beating and probably a stomping.

Moore bobbed his head. "He's a troublemaker all right. There's only one way to handle that kind. Not your way. You'd tear Charley's place up. And I know Charley doesn't want that."

The man behind the bar said an emphatic, "No."

Moore grinned slowly at the circle of faces. "You were getting in each other's way. You handle them like this." Moore took a short step toward Brent.

His fist swung at the end of the step, and the momentum and the meaty shoulders gave it a powerful force. It cracked against Brent's unprotected jaw, and his conscious world exploded in a flash of red. He slipped down the bar front and sprawled limply on the floor.

He didn't see Moore rub his knuckles, nor hear him say, "Like that. Nice and easy. A night in jail and a stiff fine will teach him some manners. Charley, put the next round on my bill."

Broken Bit crowded around him, mauling and whacking him. He avoided their insistence that he drink with them by saying, "I might be back. Right now, I've got work to do."

He went out of the door dragging Brent behind him.

2

MOORE WAS sitting with his feet propped up on the desk when Haymes came in. Haymes was a stoop-shouldered man with defeat written heavily on his face. Sagging was the only word to describe him. His face sagged, and his body sagged. He was a futile man but an able politician. A man could always find him in the saloons, buying a drink where it would do him the most good.

He looked at the cell behind the office. "Who you got there?"

Moore shrugged. "Some breed. Drunk and disorderly."

"You fine him and get him out of here. Get him out before breakfast." Haymes' anger built. "Damn it, Lucas. I'll bet he hasn't got a dime in his pockets. He can't pay a fine. I'm not putting out good money to feed a worthless breed. Why didn't you dump him in the river?"

Moore gave him an easy grin. "I'll take care of him."

"I don't want him here when I come in in the morning."

"He won't be."

"He'd better not be." Haymes turned for the door. "I'll be at the Bull's Head if you want me."

Sure, Moore thought, as he watched Haymes leave. I can find you in one saloon or another.

He dropped his feet to the floor and walked to the cell. His eyes were concerned. Brent was still out. The concern left his eyes as Brent stirred and groaned.

He moved to the water cooler, dipped out a cupful, and came back to the cell. He opened the unlocked door, walked to Brent's side, and splashed some of the water into his face.

Brent's eyes opened, and he groaned again as he tried to sit up.

13

Moore helped him with his free hand. He imagined Brent's head was pounding like hell. He waited until his prisoner's eyes cleared. As the vagueness left Brent's eyes, they grew bitter and malevolent. Moore handed him the rest of the water.

Brent's eyes never left Moore's face as he drank it. They were wild eyes, burning with a single purpose. "You bastard. I could kill you."

Moore grinned cheerfully. "I expect you could." His face hardened. "Which did you want? One quick punch from me? Or the going over they would've handed you?"

"You know I didn't start it."

Moore nodded. "Sure."

The wildness in Brent was growing. "But I end up in jail. You heard what they called me. I'm in jail because of what I am."

"You're feeling good and sorry for yourself, aren't you? I've had my eye on you for some time. I thought you were man enough to do a job. Maybe I was wrong." Now his words sounded angry. "Why do you think I busted you and dragged you down here? So I could talk to you without interruption. Where else could I pick and not run the risk of somebody interrupting it?"

Some of the murky rage in Brent's eyes changed to bewilderment. This talk had taken a tangent that had lost him.

Moore fixed him with hard eyes. "I know all about you. You're a quarter North Piegan. Your father ran out on your mother shortly before you were born. I don't know where he is, and it doesn't matter. You've grown up blaming everything bad that's happened to you on your Indian blood. Maybe you've been begging for the kicking around you've been getting. A man without self-respect invites it."

The wild glare came back to Brent's eyes. It was all right for Moore to talk this way. He hadn't taken the abuse.

"Did you hate your mother, too? She was half Indian."

Brent's eyes widened. God no, he didn't hate her. She was the only thing tender and loving he had ever known. She had died of smallpox five years ago, when he was fifteen, and even now those days of grief rushed back at him so vividly that he relived them.

"She wasn't ashamed of her blood. Neither was your grandmother."

14

Brent didn't remember his grandmother very well. She had been old and wrinkled by the time he'd reached the age of comprehension.

"Maybe you've been ashamed of the wrong blood all this time. I never knew an Indian to break his promise. I can't say that for a lot of white men I've known. Did you ever stop to think that the white man made the Indian the way he is? He took the pride from him; he turned him into a drunken, shuffling wreck. He took his way of living from him and gave him nothing in return. He killed or drove the game out of the country, and you expect the Indian to keep his dignity while he's starving. So he steals and gets drunk, and you blame him."

Brent was growing more confused. Why was Moore telling him all this? "You sound like an Indian."

"No," Moore corrected. "I think like one. I happen to think he's a man and should be allowed to walk like one. I talked to Charlot, chief of the Flatheads, after James Garfield forged Charlot's name to a treaty Charlot refused to sign because of its unfairness. I've never forgotten his words. 'Who sent him here?' Charlot asked. 'We were happy when he first came. We first thought he came from the light, but he comes like the dusk of the evening now, not like the dawn of the morning. He comes like a day that has passed, and night enters our future with him. He comes as long as he lives and takes more and more, and dirties what he leaves.'" Moore paused reflectively. "And by God, it's true."

Brent's head swam in a lot of words, and it ached too much to sort them out.

"I haven't convinced you of anything yet, have I? The white man brought the Indians two things that can wipe him out entirely. Smallpox and whiskey. I think whiskey's the worst. It's illegal, but it flourished more than ever." His eyes were hard and shiny. "If I could have my pick of doing one thing, that would be it. Stamp out the whiskey trade."

He grimaced and shook his head. "I guess I get pretty worked up over it. I don't know why an Indian can't handle alcohol as well as a white man. Some of the eastern tribes used ceremonial intoxicants made from herbs or vegetables and did themselves little harm. But the northwest Indians never used it. The white man put unlimited quantities in their

15

hands, and as long as they have access to it, it's going to mean nothing but misery to themselves and everybody else. The Hudson Bay Company started it, though they were never as greedy for profits as the Americans. We've refined the business, we've really brought it up to a high degree of efficiency. It's a profitable thing. An active whiskey post can easily net twenty thousand dollars a year. It's estimated that twenty-five thousand gallons were distributed to a hundred and twenty thousand Indians last year. Our politicians make speeches about the evils of it, they pass laws against it, and they might as well try to club a man to death with a rolled-up newspaper. Everything they've done is useless unless they see that the laws are enforced. You arrest a whiskey trader and bring him into court, and he's turned loose for lack of evidence. Even though you bring in a wagonload of it with him."

He paced back and forth. "You're wondering why I'm telling you all this? I'm giving you a chance to be part of something that can put some pride in you."

He pulled a badge out of his pocket. He tossed it to Brent, and Brent caught it. He looked at it, then raised his head and stared at Moore. The embossed letters read, *Deputy U. S. Marshal.*

Moore's eyes had an intentness that was like a fire. "A dozen good men have been here trying to stamp out the traffic. Then we thought we'd try a new angle. If I didn't come here openly as a marshal, I might be able to get a line on who's behind it." His face had a raw, wicked look. "That's the man, or men, I want. It takes big money to finance the trade. I want the man who supplies that money." He drew a deep breath. "Are you going to help me find him?"

He saw the refusal forming in Brent's face. "All right. But I thought you'd like to do something for your mother's people. I thought you'd like a job that would let you walk tall again." His laugh scraped like a dull razor. "Go back and pick up your ax."

Brent's face was sullenly angry. "What the hell could I do?"

"You could make the difference. I can deputize you. And see that you're supplied with a horse and gun. You won't make much money, but it'll be steady. You can't wave your badge around, but you'll know it's in your pocket. Damn it, if that doesn't lift your head, nothing will."

The offer beckoned to Brent. It offered an escape from the drudgery of a job that gave him nothing but a miserable existence. Twenty minutes ago not even the wildest of his thoughts could have imagined something like this. "Why, I wouldn't even know where to start."

Moore's eyes had a new shine. "I don't either. All we can do is to stumble along until we fall into something. It'll probably be dangerous." He saw no reaction in Brent's face to that. "We can't legally go into Canada. And most of the whiskey-trading posts are across the line. Even if we could raid them, we'd be stamping on the tail of the snake instead of the head. Brent, find that head for me."

The ache in Brent's head was diminishing, or perhaps he was too excited to notice it. "What do I do first?"

"I want you to get a job with Broken Bit." Moore grinned at the startled expression on Brent's face. "Sounds like I'm throwing you to the wolves, doesn't it? But after I talk to Church Dawes, I think he'll keep them off of you. Particularly when I tell him you might be able to stop some of his cattle losses. He's going crazy under them. Or maybe it's a part of his mask. I've got to know. We're not doing any good chasing whiskey wagons. I've raced too many of them trying to get across the border. Maybe they're sneaking through Broken Bit land. It takes a lot of wagons to keep the trading posts in Canada supplied. Fort Slide-out, Stand-off, and Whoop-up. If I can cut off their supplies, they'll die. See if you can find out if it comes off of Broken Bit. It doesn't fit Dawes, but he's big enough to head it up. He's only the first of a list I have in mind. It's going to take time to check them out, but I don't know how else to go about it. You'll be pretty free looking for lost or stolen cattle. Keep your eyes open, and maybe you'll make that lucky stumble."

Brent still held the badge in his hand. Slowly, he slipped it into his pocket.

Moore nodded with satisfaction. "I saw Dawes in town earlier this evening. Maybe he's still here. If not, I'll ride out and talk to him in the morning. Can I get you anything before I go?"

Brent shook his head. He wished he were starting anyplace

but Broken Bit. It didn't take much imagination to see some rough hours ahead. He would be taking Dawes' money while he worked against him. That didn't bother him. He had no reason to love a cattleman.

A thought checked Moore's move toward the door. "You eaten tonight?"

Broken Bit had interrupted Brent's plans for supper. And he had been to absorbed listening to Moore to think about it. His stomach growled at him as he shook his head.

"I'll bring something back when I come." Moore closed the cell door behind him. "It's not locked. If you change your mind, you can still run."

Brent looked steadily at him. He wouldn't run. For the first time in a long while, he had the feeling of belonging to something.

Moore grinned. "I didn't think you would."

He walked outside and looked up and down the street. Asking at the hotel would be the fastest way of learning whether or not Dawes was still in town.

He stepped into the small, dirty lobby. Mud had been tracked in until he couldn't see the cracks in the floor. And it wouldn't be swept out until Pardee was thoroughly sure the rain had stopped for a long while. Pardee was a frugal man with everything, and that included work.

Pardee was dozing behind the desk. He lifted a thin, sallow face at Moore's question and yawned. He was stoop-shouldered, with a dispirited air about him. Moore wouldn't have his job. All the tomorrows would be exactly like the days gone by. Pardee would grow thinner and more turned in on himself. Every man had a choice. Some didn't make much use of it.

Pardee glanced at the bank of pigeon holes behind him. "His key's here. I guess he's in his room."

"Thanks." Moore started for the stairs.

"Is Church in trouble?"

Moore stopped and looked at the malicious gleam in Pardee's eyes. "Why, no. No trouble at all."

He chuckled silently at the disappointment in Pardee's eyes and climbed the stairs. He rapped on the door of room 107, and an impatient, gruff voice called, "It isn't locked."

Moore entered the room. Church Dawes sat on the bed,

tugging on a boot. He was in his undershirt, and the top three buttons were open, exposing a mat of thick, grizzled hair.

"Pull this damned thing off for me." He didn't ask. Church Dawes never asked. He demanded.

"You shouldn't be so damned vain and buy boots to fit your feet."

Dawes wasn't noted for his sense of humor. He bristled until he saw Moore's grin.

"They're too damned new." He extended a leg.

Moore straddled the leg and put his butt toward Dawes. He took hold of the boot, and Dawes put a foot against his butt. Even with all that leverage the boot came off hard.

Moore helped him off with the other one and watched Dawes wriggle his toes in relief. "You're not getting your fair share out of life, Church."

Dawes gave him a suspicious glance. "What's my fair share?"

"A few drinks and loose boots." Moore chuckled.

"Did you climb these stairs just to tell me that?"

"I wanted to talk to you." Moore took the only chair in the room and eased his weight into it. A man was foolish to trust these hotel chairs too far.

It was a bare little room with its iron bedstead, the single chair, and the washstand with its chipped pitcher and bowl. The green blind at the window was cracked and peeling. Dawes could afford better. Fort Benton just didn't have any better.

Dawes was still a powerful man, though age was beginning to turn his muscles stringy and loosen his face. He had as cold an eye as Moore had ever seen. His eyes stared out at a man from under a briar patch of bristling brows. Moore could admire his determination but not always his method. Dawes came from Texas, and he had been one of the first to drive his herd up the Bozeman Trail. He had carved out an empire by sheer drive and unbendable will. He didn't fit the picture of a whiskey trader, but if he had gone into it, Moore knew he would make a success of it.

"You've seen me before," Dawes said testily. "Get on with it."

He was a hard, unbending man, and Moore wished he

knew just how honest he was. "You ought to be grateful to me, Church. I could've thrown your boys in jail."

Dawes snorted. "For what? For trying to teach a breed some manners? Daggett told me about it."

Daggett was Dawes' foreman, and Moore didn't like the man. Daggett used his standing to rub against the grain, and his eyes were mean.

"Church, how are you getting along with Major Argenbright?" He deliberately hit Dawes on a festering wound, and he knew what would follow.

Dawes cursed the Major until he was breathless. "The goddam worthless army," was only a small part of it. He exploded at Moore's grin. "You tell me what good they are. They can't even handle their own beef herd. Every time they go out to cut out a head, they stampede the herd. Then they come yelling to the ranchers to get it back for them. Argenbright's lucky. He's got enough cattlemen and settlers around here to protect him and his troops. You tell me one thing he's done. Has he stopped the Indians stealing our cattle?"

He reached under the bed and pulled out a bottle to refuel his anger. He lowered its level a measurable distance to the eye and recorked it. He put it back without offering it to Moore.

"Are you still losing stock?" Moore knew he was, but he wanted to prod Dawes' anger to a greater pitch. As perverse as the man was, it could make him amenable to what Moore had in mind.

"You know damned well I am. Do you know what that army does? If by blind luck they recover stolen stock and capture the Indians, they escort them back to the reservation. The stock disappears damned quick there. And we're not allowed to go on the reservation after it. We've asked the army to order the Indian agents to stop giving permits for the Indians to leave the reservation. Request refused. Then we asked to have the troops stationed at points along the trails the Indians use, as a warning to them. Request refused. The War Department did give us permission to report Indians on our range known to be raiding. Now ain't that a hell of a lot?"

Moore shook his head in sympathy. Dawes' indictment was true.

"All they're good for is to hold their balls or give amateur readings. The best news I've heard come out of the post is when I read last week a cavalryman fell off a horse and broke his neck." He glowered at Moore. "I've got a bellyful. I'm about ready to take things in my own hands."

"That's what I came up to talk to you about. I've got a man who knows this country like the back of his hand. And he knows Indians. If he spent full time looking around, he might come up with something interesting."

"Who is he?"

"That breed your men were roughing around."

Dawes howled his indignation. "I got no more use for a damned Indian than I have for the army."

"Suit yourself." Moore pushed off his chair. "He's a quarter Indian. Just enough to have Indian savvy. But you go right ahead and chase around in circles."

He saw the wavering in that craggy old face and waited.

"He's a good man?"

"None better."

"I might give him a try. Send him out. But by God, he'd better produce."

Moore sighed inwardly. It was entirely possible that nobody would get any good out of this. But at least Brent would have a chance to check out Broken Bit and Church Dawes.

"Tell your men to keep off of him."

Dawes' face mottled with anger. "If you think I'm going to wet-nurse some damned breed—" He wavered under the relentless impact of Moore's eyes. "All right. I'll keep them off him. But he'd better do a job for me."

"He will." Moore walked to the door. He had set a wheel in motion. He didn't know what kind of ground it was going to run over, but at least it was moving.

3

BRENT DIDN'T leave Fort Benton until well into the afternoon of the following day. Maybe it was because of an uneasiness he wouldn't admit, or maybe he had wasted time in the pure delight of having money to spend.

He had bargained hard with Cleary, the livery-stable man, over a big flashy bay. He had seemingly let Cleary convince him of how much more value there was in the animal over anything else in the corral. Cleary went on underrating the other horses, apparently believing Brent was sold on the bay.

"You take that little knotheaded piebald." He scornfully pointed at the animal. "The bay is three times the horse."

The piebald was ewe-necked and it stood droop-headed. But it had a wary, watchful eye with a degree of meanness in it. Brent had seen these little knotheads before. They were short on looks but long on endurance.

"I'll buy the piebald." He offered a third of the price Cleary had quoted on the bay.

Cleary blinked, then grinned sourly. "That was the one you were after all the time, wasn't it?"

At Brent's admission, Cleary had said, "I'll stick to my price. You made a buy."

Brent thought so. The farther he rode the animal, the more he thought it. The piebald had a waspish temper, but they would get along as long as Brent never made the mistake of getting careless around it.

He wore a new outfit and a pair of boots. At each place of purchase he had used the story Moore advised. He had hit a poker game a good lick. Nobody had questioned the story.

He had ridden past Moore lounging in the doorway of Haymes' office, and Moore had given no indication that he had even seen him.

Broken Bit lay twelve miles from Fort Benton, and Brent put the piebald to a steady lope. His thoughts were busy and apprehensive. Moore had said everything was going to be all right, but that was no guarantee of how Broken Bit would receive him. But nothing chained him to Church Dawes. If he didn't like what he found out there, it was a simple matter of riding away from the place.

The piebald kept up that effortless stride. Twenty more minutes would see him there. The road made an abrupt turn, and a hundred yards after coming out of it, a buggy was down and tilted precariously in the road.

A woman, her back toward Brent, stood looking at the road-bound axle. She had lost a wheel, and it must have been a severe jar when that axle went down. The axle end had gouged the road, and she was fortunate the buggy hadn't overturned.

Her hands were on her hips, and she appeared more angry than hurt. He slowed the piebald to a walk, and faint snatches of her words drifted to him. He grinned at them. "Damn it. Oh, damn it." She was angry all right.

The sound of the approaching hoofs cut through her anger, and she turned and looked up at him.

She pointed at the axle. "Look at that damned thing."

His tongue was suddenly thick and clumsy. He couldn't say if her hair was a light black or a dark auburn. It depended upon how the sun caught it. Her eyes were green, flecked with gold—strange, fascinating eyes—and he had the feeling they would change every time her moods changed. Her face was more expressive than beautiful, but it had an attraction no man could fail to notice. She had something that was better than outward beauty. She had an inner vitality, a radiance, and it crackled now like leaping flames. She was as lithe as a willow branch but still noticeably woman. She handled her hands gracefully, and he imagined all her movements would be like that. He judged her to be somewhere around his age. He was staring, and he couldn't help it.

She frowned at him. "Can't you talk?"

He felt his face heat. "Are you hurt?"

"Do I look like it? Are you going to just sit there?"

"No, Ma'am." He slid to the ground. The imperative note in her voice showed that she was used to commanding. He wasn't her man, and she had better take that ordering out of her tone.

He scowled at her. "Did you see where the wheel went?" A wheel coming off like this one had would have enough momentum to travel quite a way.

Some kind of laughter glinted in her eyes at the change in him. "Where you going to look for it?"

That glint made him uneasy. He had the feeling she was readying some kind of trap for him.

"I'll have to find it and bring it back. When I lift the buggy, you can slip it on." This was the place to cut her down. "Or were you thinking of driving the buggy to it?"

"I couldn't drive without the wheel, could I?" She sounded

sweet and submissive. "But after the wheel was on, I was wondering what was going to hold it there. I thought maybe we ought to find the nut first before we do all that other work."

His face was hot. By not thinking of that, he had stepped squarely into her trap. A cutting down had happened, but it had gone the wrong way.

She went into a peal of laughter at his expression. His resentment grew as he listened to it. She was a perverse, headstrong female. It wasn't hard to decide he didn't like her.

"Yes," he growled, and stalked back down the road. It was probably a useless search. A wheel could stay on an axle quite a way after a nut slipped off, and the nut would have to be in the middle of the road for him to spot it. If it had rolled to the side of the road, he would never see it among the weeds.

She joined him in the search, and he kept his eyes riveted on the road. The little tinkles of laughter that came from her didn't help his outraged feelings a bit.

After a quarter of a mile he decided the search was useless. He didn't know how the piebald would react to carrying her, but he had to make the offer.

"I don't think we'll find it," he said stiffly. "I can give you a lift to where you can get more help." He didn't want to be in her company a moment longer than was necessary.

"That damned Church," she exploded. "Giving me a buggy that's unsafe to drive."

He had a stupid look on his face. "Church Dawes?" He knew it was. He had never heard of another Church.

"My father." She looked at him with more-open interest. "If you're looking for a job, he's full-up."

"I've already got a job with him." He tried to shrivel her. She knew too many answers; she needed putting in her place.

Laughter danced in her eyes, but her tone was meek enough. "I'm glad."

He wouldn't accept nor trust that tone. He led the piebald to her and said, "We'll have to take it easy and see how he behaves. He's got some mean in him."

"I couldn't have you walk."

He was suspicious of the dismay in her voice. "It's all right—"

"Particularly when it isn't necessary. I was getting ready to unhitch Blackie when you came up."

The laughter in her eyes mocked him again, and he swore at himself. He hadn't thought straight from the moment he saw her. She made him feel like a damned fool, and he wanted to yell at her. Sometimes a buggy horse wasn't a riding horse, and he didn't care. She had trampled him enough, and he wouldn't offer anything, including suggestions. He wouldn't offer to unharness the horse or to give her a lift up.

She went into that fingernailed laughter again, and he could feel it scraping him good. "I'm sorry," she gasped. "But if you could see how you look." She choked off another burst and thrust out her hand. "Friends?"

She could veer so fast, a man couldn't begin to keep his balance. He didn't want to take that hand, he didn't want to forgive her.

A reluctant smile tugged at his mouth corners. She had an infectious charm when she wanted to use it, and he couldn't keep the smile from spreading. He took the hand. "I guess I looked and sounded pretty foolish."

She couldn't keep her laughter bottled up, and he found himself joining in it.

"No," she denied. "You were a noble white knight, offering to help a lady in distress."

He didn't know what a white knight was, but the way she said it didn't sound bad.

"I was mad at the buggy and mad at Church. I took it out on you. It's a bad habit I learned from Church."

Suddenly he felt lighthearted and gay. He unhitched the horse, and Blackie was a docile animal, for he showed no alarm at a stranger.

Brent laid the harness in the buggy and looped and tied the long reins so she could handle them. He helped her up, and she sat as though she were riding sidesaddle.

She smiled at his dubious expression. "I've ridden Blackie like this before."

He kept the pace to a slow walk, and she asked a lot of questions about him. He decided her interest was genuine,

25

and he didn't evade many of the questions. He carefully refrained from asking anything about her. She was only being kind, and he was a fool if he tried to make more out of it.

Once peace was established between them, she chattered like magpie. Her first name was Paula, and she was nineteen years old. Her mother had died six years ago. A momentary sadness touched her face when she said that. She lived with her father and grandmother, and she had been away to school in the East for a year. She would never go back. All those buildings stifled her.

She cocked her head at him. "You don't talk much, do you?"

"No," he agreed. He guessed he had gotten out of the habit.

"We'll change that."

She sounded as though she expected the association to continue. She was wrong.

Her hand swept out toward the cluster of buildings just coming into view. "Home."

He looked at the house with curiosity. It was a strictly utilitarian shelter built of split and chinked logs. It looked sturdy and unshakable against any kind of weather Montana might throw at it, and that was the important thing.

A similar building, only longer, lay behind it, and he guessed that was the bunkhouse. His face hardened as he remembered bad times in other bunkhouses.

She caught the expression and her eyes sobered, but she didn't question him about it. She was an odd mixture of girl-child and adult woman. At the moment she had the perception of the woman.

Dawes was out in front of the house as they rode up, and he put a frown on Brent. He didn't know what had happened, but the frown said he didn't like it.

She talked first. "This is Brent Bargen. And don't you jump him. The wheel came off of that damned buggy. I'd be sitting out there yet if he hadn't come along."

Brent hid his grin. That was a lie, but it made for a powerful attack on her father. She glanced at Brent, and there was a twinkle in her eyes. She was getting him off to a good start by making Dawes grateful to him.

26

Her attack put Dawes on the defensive. "How did I know that wheel was coming off?"

"You could have those wheel nuts checked once in a while." She slid to the ground and walked by him, her face unforgiving.

Dawes watched her until she disappeared into the house, and there was a softness in his face. It said how much this girl meant to him.

The softness was gone when he looked at Brent. "I appreciate what you did for her. Don't try to use it."

Brent stared stonily at him, and Dawes returned the stare. Brent wondered at the instant hostility that had sprung up between them.

"Moore says you're a good man. I expect to see some results. That's the bunkhouse. You can put your horse in the corral."

It was a curt dismissal; it also drew a line between the hands' quarters and the ranch house.

He untied his war bag and dumped it on the ground. He stripped saddle and bridle from the horse and turned it into the corral.

He shouldered his war bag and walked into the bunkhouse. Sandy and three other riders were inside. He didn't know the three by name, but he remembered their faces. The last time he had seen them, they had been angry faces behind the punches thrown at him.

Sandy's face filled with pleasure. "Well, well. Now I get me the chance to find out something that's been rankling me."

Brent stared at him blank-faced, but the queasiness was rolling in his stomach. He wasn't going to be allowed a minute of peace.

"I figure you called me a name, Indian. I want to hear what it was."

Brent's lips were stiff. "Mr. Dawes hired me." He hoped it would keep Sandy off of him.

Sandy pretended astonishment. "I'd have thought the old man had better sense than that. You tell me how that figures in what's between you and me." He advanced in little stalking steps, and the three followed him.

Brent wasn't going to retreat, and he wasn't going to take

a beating. Words wouldn't do a damned bit of good, and his fists weren't enough to take four of them. But he had a gun at his hip.

A voice thundered from the doorway, "Stop it."

Dawes came into the room, and his face was furious. "What's this all about?"

"It's kind of personal business, Church," Sandy answered.

"I'm making it my business. I hired this man to do a special job. And I want it done. You bother him, and you'll answer to me. Is that understood?"

Their eyes broke before his hard gaze. "Hell, Church—"

"You don't listen very well, do you, Sandy?"

"I listen good," Sandy said hastily. He swung malevolent eyes toward Brent. He had been called down publicly, and it made another item to add to his score.

He stalked past Dawes, and the other three put uneasy eyes on Dawes before they followed him.

That might have been contempt in Dawes' eyes. "They won't bother you. Supper in twenty minutes."

Brent felt no gratitude toward the man. Dawes hadn't stepped in out of any sense of charity. "I'm not hungry."

"Suit yourself." Dawes walked out of the building.

Brent unrolled a mattress on a bunk and stretched out on it. He locked his hands behind his head and stared at the ceiling. He wished he had never listened to Moore. Finding Dawes in the middle of the whiskey trade wouldn't bother him; in fact, it might wipe out some of the contempt he had seen in Dawes' eyes. But there was a girl involved in it, a girl who had taken a subtle hold on him.

He swore softly and changed his position. He had a pretty good inkling he wouldn't find any comfort so long as he remained at Broken Bit.

4

MacLendon Nader stood at the window of his office and watched the traffic flow by in the street. Nader wasn't his real name, but he had forced himself to forget his real one.

28

Not only was it dangerous to him, but it belonged to a time and country to which he could never return. This was rough, savage land, and his lip curled as he thought of what it had to offer a gentleman. He was a gentleman, he thought fiercely. He clung to that distinction though here it had no meaning.

Nostalgia touched him as it always did when he thought of that better time. Then people knew how to live graciously. The war between the states had destroyed all that. How well he remembered his supreme confidence at the start of it. In a week's time the blue-bellies would be fleeing in all directions.

His face was frozen as he thought of how wrong he had been. He had risen to the rank of colonel, but at the war's end it was an empty title. It wouldn't buy a man a crust of bread, and he had little else to use.

He had lived by his wits, and he felt no regrets over any part of it. He had seen the woman ride by in a carriage and made note of the richness of her attire. Her eyes had rested on him a long moment, and he had correctly interpreted the message.

Clarissa had been the wife of an important carpetbagger, bored and frustrated with her life in a southern city. He wasn't sure who had seduced whom, and his lips moved in a cold smile. But she had let him live in somewhat the manner he was accustomed to. He would have been content to go on with the arrangement indefinitely, but in some manner her husband had found out about it.

The fool had given him no warning. He had jerked out a pistol one afternoon and fired at point-blank range on the main street. The ugly whisper of the bullet at his ear was still vivid. He had cooly shot the man between the eyes, then fled. A plea of self-defense wouldn't have saved him, not with a pack of angry carpetbaggers clamoring for his hide. She had furnished him the money and a horse for his escape, and he had promised to send for her.

His chuckle held a note of malice as he wondered if she was still waiting.

He pulled out a gold-cased watch. Where was that fool Daggett? He should have been here thirty minutes ago.

Nader's eyes were vicious. Daggett was getting too independent for his own good.

His mind went back to the past. He had made his way through Louisiana and into Texas. He had let his beard grow and worn soiled, ragged clothing. Nobody would ever have associated him with the man they once knew, but he couldn't take the chance of remaining in Texas. It was Yankee-dominated land, and a stray glance or the wrong word could pinpoint him for official attention.

He had made his way north into a country he detested, a harsh country of deep snows and chilling blasts. He was trained for no special work, and he found the living hard. He had been caught up in the various rushes to the gold camps, and an eager hope was always with him. One strike, one lucky strike, and he would be back living the way he should. He had never made that strike. Other men did, and his bitterness increased each time he heard of it. He had worked until his hands were raw and bleeding, he had stood in icy water hour after hour, and that strike always evaded him.

How well he remembered the night he had been trudging back to town, his spirit and will defeated. He had caught up with an old man, and the old man had been jubilant. He had made his strike, he was carrying five thousand dollars in gold on him, and there was more where that came from.

Nader remembered his agony at the news. What good would the strike do the old man? All the juices of life were dried up in him, and the money could bring him no enjoyment. A murderous rage had seized him as he listened to the old man's babbling.

"I'm going to live good from now on," the old man had crowed.

Nader knew what he was going to do before his hand touched his pistol. "But not for long, my friend," he said as he shot him.

The man's eyes had been filled with animal pleading as he fell. It hadn't touched him then and hadn't bothered him since.

He had hidden the body well, and no one had been interested enough to make prolonged inquiries. He had made one stupid mistake, and he still excoriated himself whenever he thought of it. He hadn't found out the location of the strike before he shot the man.

But that five thousand had served him well. He had built successfully on it until today he owned this bank and the respect it entailed. And there was far more wealth and respect ahead for him. Give him another two years in the whiskey-trading business, and he would have so much money that nothing could catch him. There was no doubt this territory would soon become a state. And the people of it would look to men of wealth and standing for their leaders. It meant Washington and a civilized life again. At times the longing for that was a physical ache.

He had left no footprints in his climb. He had seized each opportunity as it came along, used it for his gain, then tossed it away. And no man could point a finger at him and say, you were behind that one. This latest venture was as successfully hidden. The alcohol from St. Louis was consigned to another name, and other men delivered it to Fort Whoop-up. The profits were tremendous, though he always raged at the occasional loss of his - wagons. The damned moralists were always interfering in a man's life. Who cared what happened to a bunch of filthy savages? The quickest way to get rid of them was to let them get drunk and kill each other off.

He had only one lack—a woman. Not any woman and certainly not the painted chippies who could be found in Fort Benton. No, it had to be one certain woman, and so far she hadn't given much indication that she knew he was alive. That hard, aching knot in his belly; it was always there when he thought of Paula Dawes. She was only half his age, but that didn't matter. Her wild, flaming spirit had gripped him from the moment he knew it. It needed subduing, and he was the man for that. He would take her to Washington with him; he would give her the kind of life in which she could blossom.

He walked to the mirror on the far wall and stared at his reflection. Certainly there was vanity in him, and who had a better right to it? He was still a fine figure of a man, tall and lean, and elegantly dressed, though his waistband was beginning to tighten. He patted his stomach and frowned. He would have to watch his eating a little more. He had blond hair, and thirty years from now he would look much the same. Blond-headed men wore better than dark-headed ones. He stroked the blond beard. He would probably shave it off now, but he was used to it, and caution still dictated his steps. He wondered if she would notice him more if he was clean-shaven, and rage seized him. She would notice him. He had been patient with her, but that could come to an end. His hold was increasing on Church Dawes. Dawes could walk in here and get whatever money he needed. One of these days, and soon, he would close his fist on Dawes. He flattered himself that Dawes wouldn't object to his suit too much.

He turned from the mirror. Things were going as he had hoped, and he would not let impatience force him into a hasty step.

He snapped his head around at the knock on the rear door. That would be Daggett. It was about time he showed up. "Come in," he called.

His face mirrored his displeasure as Holt Daggett came into the room. He would have to ride hard to avoid being late for his invitation to supper at Broken Bit.

"Don't jump me," Daggett said. "It took longer to load the wagons than I figured."

He was a heavy-faced man with dull dark eyes. His neck was cross-hatched with weather wrinkles, and he never seemed to know quite what to do with his hands.

Nader's contempt was in his eyes. Daggett was a clod, but he had his uses. If this thing ever blew up, he was one of the few links connecting MacLendon Nader to it, and those links could be removed. He knew where Daggett had spent that time. He was infatuated with Molly Sanders, that blonde chippy at the Bull's Head saloon, and he spent as much time as he could get and all of his money on her. Nader didn't care as long as it didn't interfere with his business. He knew Daggett needed money before he had proposed this to him, and Daggett had grabbed eagerly at it. He had wanted to quit his job with Dawes, but Nader wouldn't let him. He could operate longer and more safely as long as suspicion didn't touch him. Daggett took the raw alcohol, loaded it on the wagons, and sent them north. It took an animal cunning just getting the wagons across the border. Once they were across, the worries were practically over. For as long as the government of Canada was content to keep no organized law

32

north of the border, the wagons could roll with impunity. And for that, Nader paid him well.

He nodded in forgiveness. It took tremendous sums to finance this, and Daggett kept things rolling for him. The individual traders, dispensing whiskey out of a single wagon from an overnight camp, were minor competition, but more of an annoyance rather than serious competition. And if they kept at it long enough, the Indians took care of them for him. The Indians hated a whiskey trader. It was almost as though they had enough intelligence to realize what the trader was doing to them. They couldn't resist trading with him, but if they caught him alone on the prairie, they put enough arrows into him to turn him into a pincushion. Nader gave little more consideration to the other whiskey forts. They weren't as well organized as he was, and he could forgive Daggett some of his blundering clumsiness because he kept that organization going.

"Daggett, I heard from Whoop-up. They're running low on alcohol. Are the wagons ready to go?"

"They'll move tonight."

Nader nodded his satisfaction. At Whoop-up the alcohol would be watered down and mixed with other ingredients that gave it the kick the Indian liked. It made a vile, nauseous mess, and only a savage could stomach it. He knew of white men who drank trade whiskey. He put them in the same class as the Indians.

"Wait here for ten or fifteen minutes," he ordered. He allowed himself to be seen with Daggett as little as possible. He disliked the man's company in the first place, and in the second, not being seen with him minimized the danger of somebody connecting them.

Daggett nodded. "Sure, boss."

That cold smile was on Nader's face as he left the room. Daggett wouldn't even use a chair in Nader's office. He would stand all that time. The thought pleased Nader. He liked dominion over all things in his life.

He walked to the livery stable and waited impatiently while old Amos saddled and brought out the sorrel. A rare warmth came into his eyes as he looked at it. It had the sleek look of being well cared for. It should. He paid the old man enough. He pressed a bill into Amos' hand and relished the fawning regard he received in return.

He mounted and rode out of town at a canter. He cut a fine figure on a horse, and people turned to watch him. They gave him the same kind of regard Amos did, and this was only the beginning.

Outside of town he put the sorrel into a run, and its thoroughbred blood showed. He owned the best horse for miles around, and he accepted it as his due. That stupid Argenbright had tried to buy it from him, and he snorted at the thought of how the dumpy major would look on this animal. The horse put a shine in Paula's eyes, and when things were settled between them, he would give it to her. He could give her so many things if she only had the sense to listen to him.

He let the sorrel run until it showed the first faint signs of distress. Then he stopped to let it blow. He never abused a fine horse.

He rode empty-handed this evening because she had refused little gifts in the past. She was as elusive as a puff of smoke, and the thought of that elusiveness made him set his teeth. He would wait a little longer before he started applying subtle pressure.

He rode into the yard, and Dawes was outside, washing up. From the long porch back of the kitchen he could hear the babble of voices. He kept his frown from showing. They would eat with the hands again tonight. He never had any time alone with her. Church Dawes had the finer sensitivities of a hog.

Dawes finished wiping his hands on the towel hanging above the wash pan.

"Light," he said in greeting, "I was beginning to think you weren't going to make it."

Nader gave him a wry smile. "Business. Only the most urgent could keep me away."

Dawes put a sly look on his face. "I know that."

He was in accord with Nader's plans. Everybody was in accord but the only really important one. And her grandmother, Nader thought. He mustn't forget that old witch. She had never voiced a word of dislike toward him, but it was always in her eyes.

Dawes put his hand on Nader's elbow and steered him inside. The crew was eating, and only a couple of them looked up. Nader was becoming a fixture around here and wasn't worth much attention anymore.

Paula gave him a pleasant smile as he sat down. It was the kind of smile she gave everybody. She sat next to her grandmother, and she leaned over and said something to her.

Nader couldn't catch the words, but he bristled at the old crone's cackle of laughter. He had never seen Paula's mother, but Paula had to take after her instead of her grandmother. It was hard to imagine the old woman as ever having had any beauty. She was shrunken and stooped, and her skin looked as brittle and ancient as old parchment. But her black hair still retained most of its color, and her black eyes were still bright.

She felt his eyes upon her and turned her head. Those little eyes burned at him with bright malice.

Dawes looked around the table. "Daggett not here again? I don't know what the hell he's doing, but he's spending as much time at it as he is at his job."

Nader made a mental note. He would have to speak to Daggett about being gone so much. This job was an excellent mask for Daggett to work behind.

"Where's Brent?" Paula asked. "Didn't you tell him supper was ready?"

"I told him. He said he wasn't hungry."

"Is he sick?"

Nader thought that was surely a note of concern in her voice. He had to fight to keep more than a mild curiosity from his voice. "Who's this Brent?"

"Brent Bargen," Dawes answered. "I just hired him. Paula broke down on the road, and he gave her some help."

Something twisted inside Nader, and it hurt. Surely she wasn't stooping beneath her level. He marshaled his arguments to reassure himself. She wouldn't look a second time at one of the men her father hired. But Bargen had given her some kind of assistance, and that could turn a young girl's head. He cursed himself for his anxiety. He was building this up out of all proportion. But he couldn't let the matter drop—not until he knew more about this Brent Bargen.

"Church, hiring help out of gratitude is too expensive a luxury."

Dawes frowned at him. "I didn't hire him out of gratitude. I've got a special job for him. His Indian blood suits him for it. I'm tired of waiting on the army to recover stolen stock. Bargen knows the country. If he can cut their trail before they get back to the reservation, I might be able to do something about it."

Nader looked concerned. "Is that wise, Church?"

Dawes snorted. "What can the army do to me? All I'm doing is taking some work off their hands."

"I didn't mean that. I was thinking about this man's heritage. I never knew Indian blood yet that could be trusted. What's to keep him from working with them? They could steal you blind, and you'd never know it."

Dawes' face darkened at the questioning of his judgment. "Don't you think I'll be keeping an eye on him? I didn't guarantee him a lifetime job."

The grandmother had been busy stuffing food into her mouth. She ate mostly with her fingers, and Nader avoided watching her as much as he possibly could.

She stopped eating, threw back her head, and cackled in a senseless burst of merriment.

Nader's face stiffened. She wasn't looking at him, and he didn't know whether she found her amusement in him or Dawes. He forced himself to relax. Her laughter probably had no basis at all. He could put it down to senility and hit the nail on the head. My God, he had to get Paula away from this environment.

5

BRENT SAT on the top of a high hill, his elbows propped on his knees as he scanned the countryside with glasses. Ten days had been filled with nothing but this futile searching. He had found some of the trails the Indians used, but they showed no recent passage. Dawes was beginning to look at him with a sour eye, and Brent knew a brief flare of anger. What did Dawes expect, that he would manufacture a few thefts?

If Moore could see him now, he would probably have the same sour expression. For Brent had found absolutely nothing that would tie Dawes in with the whiskey trade. He was beginning to believe that Moore was wrong, and he hoped so. He admitted he enjoyed being here. In fact, he could say it was the happiest ten days he had known in a long time, even though only two people on the ranch had a civil word for him. Something was happening to him, and denying it wouldn't make it go away. He kept his contacts with Paula as brief as he could, but he couldn't deny they meant something to him. A couple of times she had asked to go with him on his daily search, and he had been wise enough to refuse. It wasn't because of his concern there might be danger for her. But he could see where this road was leading, and he had better turn off of it as quickly as he could.

Those brief contacts were filled with laughter. They could share a joke over the simplest of things. For no reason at all they would break into mutual laughter. He was sure the grandmother liked him, too. She said little, but those bright eyes were always weighing him. He wondered what they saw and pushed the thought away in quick irritation. He wished this damned job were over.

He swung the glasses in a slow sweep of the horizon, then suddenly stiffened. That was dust to his far left, and it wasn't made by the wind. It could have been made by wild animals, but it seemed too ordered and regular for that.

He kept the glasses focused on the dust, waiting for it to draw near enough for him to determine its source. His heart beat faster as the vague forms begain to solidify. Men and horses were making that dust, and they were in no hurry.

He lowered the glasses and thumbed the moisture from his eyes. He rolled them to ease them, then put the glasses back. He thought he caught a flash of blue. He would have to wait longer before he could be certain of what it was.

The little column disappeared behind the base of a hill. It seemed it took forever for them to reappear, but when they did, they were close enough for him to identify the component parts that made up the column. Twelve riderless horses were being driven ahead of it, followed by six Indians and eight troopers, carbine butts resting on their thighs. Their officer rode slack-shouldered ahead of them. Brent had heard Dawes curse often enough about this situation, and the picture was plain. The officer and troopers had captured the Indians and their stolen horses, and were escorting them back to the reservation. Dawes would be notified that his horses were on the reservation, but by the time he reached it, the horses would have disappeared.

Brent frowned in reflection. This column was headed south, and he thought the Crow reservation was their likely destination. He could do nothing by himself, but the column was proceeding at a leisurely pace. The army usually rode that way. Brent suspected there would even be a noon stop. By hard riding, he could get back to the ranch, notify Dawes, and still have time to intercept them.

He didn't spare the piebald. Gouts of foam were dropping from its muzzle by the time he hauled up beside the corral.

Dawes, Sandy, and two other riders were inside it, and they stiffened at the emergency in Brent's face.

"Saddle up," he yelled. "The army's escorting a dozen stolen horses and a half-dozen Indians toward the Crow reservation. I think we can cut them off."

Dawes needed no orders to set them into motion. Each man ran for his saddle. Brent had to have another horse, and he stripped saddle and bridle from the piebald.

Dawes pointed out a buckskin. "Take him."

Brent approved of the choice. The horse looked as though it had bottom. It was also suspicious of him, and he missed his first two throws.

He cursed his miscasts. A couple of the riders were already cinching up saddles. He coiled his rope for another throw, and a loop dropped around the buckskin's neck.

Sandy walked up the length of the rope, a malicious grin on his face. "You ain't worth much, are you?"

Brent took it with a stiff face. This was no time to push a personal argument.

He saddled the buckskin and mounted. If you pitch now, I'll break your damned head, he vowed.

The buckskin gave a tentative buck, then stopped. Dawes reined up beside Brent. "Where did you see them?"

Brent described the location, and Dawes nodded grimly. "I

know it. We've got time to cut them off. This is twelve horses I'm going to get back."

His expression worried Brent. Dawes meant what he said, even if it came to an open fight with the army.

Dawes put his horse into a full run, and the others streamed after him. It was a breakneck ride over terrain that would have scared Brent to death if he had had time to look at it closely. Dawes was evidently cutting the long angle, and he didn't slow up for anything. He raced through timber, down hills, and across rocky creeks with an utter disregard for the safety of his hide. He plunged down a long, rough slope; and the road, poorly defined, was at the base of it.

Dawes stopped at a turn in the road. "This leads to the reservation. We ought to be ahead of them."

He waved them off to the side of the road, and his face was hard as he watched that turn.

Only the heavy breathing of the horses broke the silence. Brent didn't know how much time had passed, but it seemed an eternity. He couldn't see because of that damned bend, and he kept straining his ears for sound. He was aware of the skeptical glances the others threw him, and they grew more questioning with each passing minute.

Sandy spat into the road. "Hell, he hasn't been doing enough to earn his keep. Church, he cooked this up to impress you."

Brent felt Dawes' increased hostility. If these horses didn't appear, he was in for a rough time. He could rail at the unfairness of it all he wanted to, and it would do him no good. He could point out that Dawes had led them here, that it might not even be the right road, and none of them would listen.

He thought he heard the muffled plot of a hoof and snapped, "Hold it," shutting off anything Sandy had in mind to say.

Dawes' face whipped back toward the turn. Brent heard the sound again, and Dawes said in a low voice, "Something coming."

Sandy heard it too, and he looked disappointed.

Brent didn't have to strain to catch the sounds now. They came in steady cadence, and mingled with them were the jingle of chains and the creaking of saddle leather. Brent heard a few words, followed by a burst of laughter. His tension mounted. It had to be the column he had spotted.

Dawes waved them out into the middle of the road and pulled a Winchester from its scabbard. Every man followed suit, and five rifles, their barrels resting on saddle horns, pointed at the turn.

The horses came into view first, followed by the Indians, with the troopers jamming up behind them as horses and Indians stopped. The surprise registered only in the Indians' eyes, but it was more noticeable on white faces, for jaws sagged.

A lieutenant threaded his way through the pack. He was young and new, his uniform had seen little service, and the fuzz on his cheeks hadn't begun to stiffen yet.

He looked first at the rifles, then at Dawes. "Here now. What's this?"

Dawes' face looked like eroded granite, and only the burning eyes gave it life. "You're on my land, Lieutenant. And you're driving my horses."

The lieutenant's face crimsoned. "Who are you?"

"Church Dawes. And that's my brand on those horses."

"Then you should be grateful, Mr. Dawes. The army has recovered them for you."

"Grateful, hell. I've had your kind of recovery before. Were you going to drive them to the reservation before you notified me?"

"Those are my orders, Mr. Dawes. You can place your claim there."

"I'm placing it here." Dawes lifted the rifle barrel from the horn. His face was savagely mocking. "Think of all the trouble I'm saving you."

"Get out of my way," the officer snapped, and there was too much bluster in his voice.

"You want a military funeral, Lieutenant? I heard they make big affairs out of them. The only trouble is that you won't know much about it."

The lieutenant licked his lips and glanced at his men. They stirred uneasily in their saddles, and their eyes were worried. Those five trained rifles were powerful arguments.

Brent found it difficult to breathe over the knot that had lodged in his throat. Dawes meant everything he said. Its verification was in his face, in the rifle muzzle pointed squarely at the officer's head. If the lieutenant's foolhardiness exceeded his judgment, the next few seconds would see some empty saddles.

The lieutenant's face was pale. He was caught in a spot that would have strained a more experienced man's nerves. "My orders don't cover this."

The knot in Brent's throat eased. The lieutenant had found his out.

"Take your horses, Mr. Dawes." The lieutenant's eyes could blaze now with righteous anger. "But I assure you I'll make a full report of this."

"You get those goddam red thieves off of my land." Dawes knew it was over, for his rifle lowered. "And make your report to your fat-assed major. And tell him I'll do it the same way next time. And I think the other cattlemen will handle it the same way from now on."

He turned his head. "Take 'em home, boys."

Brent joined the others in herding the horses in the direction they came from, and the troopers pulled off of the road to give them passage. Brent caught the relief in their faces. Every man here knew how that moment had teetered on a thin edge.

Dawes fell in beside Brent, and that craggy face was split in a wide grin.

"What will the army do?" Brent couldn't dismiss all of his worry. The army represented powerful authority.

"They won't do a damned thing except make a bunch of reports. By the time the reports go up to Washington and back, they'll want to forget it. Wait until I tell the other cattlemen how we pried the army's hands off my stock." He shook his head. "But for a minute back there, I didn't know."

His face was softer than Brent had ever seen it. "You did a hell of a job. You've got a job with me as long as you want it."

Sandy was close enough to hear him. "Luck. Blind, stupid luck. Anybody could—"

"Shut up," Dawes roared. "And I'm telling you for the last time. You keep your mouth off of him."

41

Sandy swept Brent with hot eyes before he spurred ahead.

Brent knew a growing contentment. He had another one on the Broken Bit who would give him a civil word. But Sandy had been right. Luck had played a part in letting him be in the right spot at the right time. A large part of that contentment was that Moore was wrong in his judgment of Dawes. Dawes was what he seemed, a hard-headed cattleman and nothing more. The next time Brent saw Moore, he would tell him so and turn in his deputy badge. He could keep this job with Broken Bit and be quite happy.

He was a big man at supper that night. Dawes insisted upon retelling the incident, and he gave Brent full credit. "He saved twelve horses for me. By God, that'll pay his salary for a long time."

Some of the other hands unbent enough to address a few words to him. Sandy stared at his plate and ate furiously. Grandmother's old eyes twinkled at Brent, and Paula had a joyous smile for him.

At the moment he rode a high horse, and only Daggett put in a jarring note. "I can use another pair of hands, Church. Why don't you turn him over to me?"

Brent waited anxiously. He didn't want that. He didn't like Daggett, and he thought the feeling was returned.

Dawes swung cold eyes toward his foreman. "You pay more attention to doing your work, and you wouldn't need more help."

Daggett colored and pushed his plate back. "I'm not very hungry tonight." Dawes never took his eyes off the man until the door slammed behind him.

Brent savored his enjoyment of the evening. Dawes was satisfied with him. He could go on the way he was. But he had picked up another enemy in Daggett. Maybe enemy was too strong, but Daggett would certainly blame him for Dawes' raking. He added up where he stood against his past position. He wanted to laugh aloud. Nobody could say he wasn't making headway.

6

BRENT PUT in long hours, casting wider and wider, hoping to duplicate his earlier success. But he wasn't under pressure now. He thought he would ask Dawes if he could go in to Fort Benton tonight. He wanted to see Moore and return that badge. He owed him some money, too, for he hadn't worked nearly long enough to pay off all that advance. But he could make that up later. He hoped Moore would understand. He was grateful for having been given his chance to step up. From the moment Moore had knocked him cold, everything had been on the mend for him. He grinned as he recalled his first outrage at Moore.

He had ridden a long way today, and if he hoped to get back to the ranch house before dark, he would have to be turning back. He wouldn't miss an evening meal if possible.

His face sobered. He knew what he had, and its bite was deep and lasting. He had no intention of trying to climb the wall between them. Just seeing her occasionally was enough to give him a sort of bittersweet satisfaction.

He swore softly as he turned the piebald. He tried to keep his thoughts from going in that direction. But they were sly snakes. Every time he grabbed one of them and tried to force it in another direction, it twisted back on him. He frowned as he thought of Nader. The man came out to Broken Bit often enough. Brent knew Paula was the reason, and he couldn't blame Nader for that. But everything in him protested it. Nader was old enough to be her father, but his intentions were plain enough. They shone in his eyes every time he looked at her. Nader's eyes were different when he looked at Brent. They were as cold as snake eyes, and they made Brent as equally uncomfortable. He just hoped Nader wouldn't be there tonight.

He rode along the rim of a coulee that drained to the south. It had been deep when he first picked it up, but now it was shelving. He put absent attention on it. Brent was tired of the endless hours of watching, with not a hoof print, either horse or cattle, to reward him.

He glanced ahead into the coulee. Against the far bank was a pile of wilting foliage. The limp and dying leaves caught his attention. They looked so out of place against the living foliage.

He dismounted opposite the pile, and excitement began to drum in his veins. Somebody had cut branches and piled them over something. And near the ground, where the branches didn't quite reach, Brent saw the partial rim of a wagon wheel.

He slipped and scrambled his way to the coulee's bottom. Why would anybody want to hide a wagon like this? He thought he knew the answer even before he moved enough branches to look into the wagon bed. A numb sickness diluted his excitement. The wagon was two-thirds loaded, and he knew what was in those rows and rows of containers even before he picked one up. He lifted it, and its contents sloshed in the jug. When he uncorked it, the final proof rose in a wave, hitting him in the face with almost physical force. This was trade whiskey, powerful enough to take the top of a man's head off.

He put the cork back and replaced the jug in its original position. He put the branches back the way they had been, and he knew he was being too meticulous. But it occupied his hands and thoughts; it kept him from thinking that Moore hadn't guessed wrong.

He climbed back to the piebald, still not sure of what he was going to do. It's her father, one voice kept saying. And another thundered in louder tones, You took Moore's money and his badge. He groaned in spiritual agony. Taking that badge was his part of a bond, and if he rode away and forgot this, he was breaking that bond.

He said a silent, I'm sorry, Paula, as his eyes roamed, picking out landmarks. He wouldn't be coming back here, but somebody else would, somebody who would need a landmark to help him find the spot.

That lightning-blasted tree was one. Its whole top had been sheered off, and most of its branches on the south side stripped away. It rose stark and naked above the other trees. A hundred yards away a granite outcropping stood baldly above the ground, and its slash of red veining made it distinctive.

He locked those things in his mind and followed the coulee. It flattened out into a tiny stream, and he followed the stream, heading in the general direction of town. He kept adding to the distinctive features of the terrain he was storing in his head.

It was well after dark by the time he reached town. He passed the sheriff's office, and Moore was inside. Moore saw him, for he nodded.

Brent kept on until he reached the end of the block, then slipped around the corner and waited. Only the saloons were lighted, but the chance of a late reveler stumbling into them was small.

He heard the slow beat of footsteps along the walk, waited until it almost reached him, and whispered, "Lucas."

Moore stopped and lit a cigarette. The flame of the match momentarily illuminated his face.

"Hello, Brent." His voice wouldn't carry three feet.

Brent told him about the wagon, and satisfaction showed in Moore's face. "So it is Dawes."

Brent's voice had a doubtful note. "I'm not positive. I didn't see him around it."

"It sounds positive enough to me, Brent. I guess it's time to quit Haymes. How do I find the wagon?"

He listened as Brent described the landmarks. "I'll find it. Somebody's going to be surprised."

Not surprised, Brent thought dully. Just sick.

"Go on back to Broken Bit, Brent, and wait until you hear from me. You may have busted this wide open. Are you going to stay in town the rest of the night?"

"I guess so."

"Do you have enough money for a room?"

"Yes."

Moore snapped the half-finished cigarette away. The talk hadn't taken long, just long enough to kill a new world for Brent.

He heard the slow beat of Moore's footsteps again and turned toward the hotel. It would be a waste of money, for he knew he wasn't going to sleep. When a man filled his head with this kind of thoughts, he knocked sleep out of it.

In the morning he looked at the slant of the sun's rays through the window and was surprised to see how late it was.

For somebody who knew he couldn't sleep, he had done pretty well.

He didn't want to go back to Broken Bit, and it was a dreary ride. Brent dreaded what he would find there, the sickness and accusation in Paula's eyes. But it couldn't happen so soon. Moore would just be reaching the wagon about now. It would still be some time before he arrested Dawes. Brent could go back and see no hatred in her eyes.

He scowled as he dismounted at the corral. Nader was here again; that was his sorrel. The scowl faded. He didn't have much right to object anymore.

After removing his saddle, he flung it across a pole, stepped out of the corral, and closed the pole gate behind him. He headed for the bunkhouse, but her voice stopped him. He stopped unwillingly and waited for her.

Laughter was in her face again. "I know you didn't have much to eat last night. Now tell me you're not hungry again." That was one of their shared jokes, his stubborn persistence of that first night.

His face and tone were harsh. "I'm not." He had to kill something, and the thought of it made him sick.

"Brent, what's wrong?"

"Nothing."

Neither tone nor expression fazed her. "Yes, there is." Her face was still and watchful. "Tell me what it is."

She tugged at his arm, and he moved unwillingly with her. She was quiet as she walked, and he wondered what words she searched for. "I'd like to know, Brent."

Her eyes were on his face, and she didn't see the small, partially embedded stone ahead of her. As her foot struck it, she tripped and was falling. But his hands flashed out and caught her. In restoring her balance, he found his face close to hers. She stared at him, and her eyes widened. He stared back, and eyes have a language more eloquent than words.

"Oh, Brent," she whispered, and her arms lifted to him.

It hadn't been planned. If he had had time, he would have refused the moment, but he was powerless against its rushing force.

His mouth sought her lips. She gave willingly, and it could have taken a second or an eternity. He broke the embrace by jerking his head away.

46

"Brent, didn't you know before?"

"No," he lied.

His tone was as brutal as a slap. It wiped the radiance from her face and put a strain in her eyes. "What is it?" She couldn't keep the quiver from her voice.

His face was a hard mask of withdrawal. "I didn't want that to happen."

"Brent!"

He forced himself to stare at her. "I mean it."

She looked at him a long moment, and her pleading was only in her eyes.

"All right, Brent." Her voice broke on his name. She whirled and ran toward the house.

He stared after her in numb misery. Her head was bent, and he was sure she was crying. He had handled it best for both of them and best for the long run. But how about right now?

Nader saw Paula slip out of the house and followed her. His eyes blazed as he saw where she was going. He would have to kill that damned breed. Neither of them saw him, and he stood close to the house until they moved away. They walked around the corral, and he followed them. He saw her stumble and Brent catch her. His anger of a moment ago was mild compared to what hit him as he saw what happened. If he had had a gun with him, he would have killed Brent on the spot.

He was too far away to hear their words, but something went wrong. He could see only her face. She said something to Brent, then whirled and ran back toward the house. She passed less than a dozen yards from him, but she didn't see him. She was crying too hard.

He flattened against the corral to keep Brent from seeing him, and his rage lessened. Something had happened between them, and perhaps he could make capital out of it. His mind pried at it from all angles. He would bring Church into this, and he was sure he could predict the man's reactions.

He found Dawes just leaving the house, and Dawes had a question that was nipping him. "What the hell happened to Paula? She went past me like a shot-scalded wolf."

Nader put the proper concern on his face. "Wasn't she crying, Church?"

Dawes looked startled. "She might have been at that. She went by too fast for me to be sure." He peered with angry attention at Nader." "Do you know something about it?"

Nader made a helpless gesture. "It's none of my business, Church. I just happened to see it."

"Get on with it."

"If you remember, I warned you about Bargen when you hired him. Paula's too young to be experienced in these matters." He paused, and his face was sorrowful.

"Goddam it," Dawes roared. "Will you tell me?"

Nader took his arm and led him a few steps from the house. "It wasn't Paula's fault. You know how friendly she is with everybody. He took advantage of it and forced his attentions on her."

Dawes' eyes turned red, and his breathing whistled. "That goddamned Indian put his hands on her?"

"You saw her crying. Why don't you ask him what happened?"

"Don't think I won't." Dawes was in the grip of a momentous rage, and Nader was satisfied. This was turning out better than he had hoped.

"Where is he?"

"The last I saw of him he was just beyond the corral."

He had to hurry to keep up with Dawes. He will kill him, Nader thought with pleasure. The pleasure slowly watered. Did he want him killed here? He was with Dawes, and Paula would blame both of them. In a young girl's mind that blame could lodge for a long time. No, it would be better if Dawes didn't go quite that far.

He pointed at the figure ahead of them. "There he is."

Brent stood with his back toward them, so absorbed that he didn't know they were near until Dawes seized his shoulder and spun him around.

"Were you out here with Paula a few minutes ago?"

Brent's eyes were harried. He could see the fury in Dawes' face, but he didn't know what was behind it. "Why, yes."

"And you put your goddamned hands on her," Dawes raved. His blow caught Brent completely by surprise. It smashed him full in the face and knocked him down. It

48

scattered his senses and watered his eyes. He felt something warm and sticky wash across his face.

"I'll kill you," Dawes panted.

He lifted a boot, and Nader thought he was going to stomp Brent. He would enjoy nothing better, but the same restraint still held him. Wouldn't it be better if Brent was just kicked off the place? He would disappear without explanation to her, and the lack of it would be a sore in her mind, festering until she hated the sound of his name.

He seized Dawes' arm and drew him back. "Church, I think he's had enough of an object lesson. Any more, and you might bring Paula into it. You don't want that."

Dawes breathed hard in the grip of his passion, but Nader's words got through to him. If this lasted longer, it would draw more attention, and everybody on the ranch would know about the mess. No, he didn't want that.

He leveled a finger at Brent and fought to control his voice. "Get off my land. If I ever see you even trying to speak to her, I'll kill you where you stand. You've got five minutes. If you're here after that, you're dead."

He turned and stamped away. Nader looked at Brent with a cold, crooked smile, then turned after Dawes. He had handled the situation beautifully, and he wouldn't appear in any part of it.

He wiped the smile from his face as he caught up with Dawes, whose anger burned as hotly as ever. "Just wait until I talk to her."

"I wouldn't, Church. I'd just let it drop. After all, it wasn't her fault. She's been embarrassed enough already."

Dawes glared at him, then his anger weakened. Nader's advice had been pretty sound in all this. Bargen would disappear, and the incident could be forgotten by everybody.

"Maybe you're right," he grumbled.

7

BRENT RODE back to town, and his spirit was dead. He hadn't tried to see Paula. Not because of Dawes' threat, but because he had hurt her enough already. The whole thing was something to be locked away in his mind and forgotten. He shook his head. He might do the first, but the second was impossible.

He stopped at Haymes' office first and asked for Moore.

"He's off on some kind of business of his own," Haymes snarled. "Did you know he's a U. S. marshal?"

Brent shook his head.

"He is. What did you want to see him about?"

Brent hunted for a quick, plausible story. "He loaned me a few dollars. I wanted to repay it."

"Damned sneaky the way he did things," Haymes fumed. "Left me shorthanded. Leave the damned money with me. I'll see he gets it."

"I'd rather give it to him."

That was the final straw, and it broke Haymes' temper wide open. "Get out of here, you damned Indian," he yelled.

Brent retreated before Haymes' wrath. Outside, he stopped helplessly. Not so long ago he had been debating a choice of roads. Now all of them had been plugged up for him. He guessed the only thing he could do was to wait for Moore's return.

He waited two days and was beginning to think Moore would never return, when he saw the big man crossing the intersection toward him.

Moore held out his hand. "Give me the makings."

He took the sack from Brent and took a deliberate time to build his cigarette. "I waited out there two days. Do you know who showed up?"

He ruined the first cigarette and threw it from him in disgust. "Daggett and Stiles. They finished loading the wagon. I waited until they drove it out of the rough country before I arrested them. I've got them locked up."

Brent felt a hollow sickness. His part in this finished him forever with Broken Bit.

"Are you going to need me as a witness?"

Moore gave him a hard appraisal. "What's wrong with you?"

Brent shook his head.

Something had hit him hard, Moore thought. His eyes probed, but he asked no questions.

"I shouldn't need you, Brent.' I've sent word to Dawes I want to see him. He'll come in. But one thing bothers me. Daggett was headed south toward the Crow reservation. Why would he be headed in that direction?"

Brent couldn't answer, and Moore muttered, "I'll find out when I talk to Dawes."

Brent thought of that tough, crusty character. It would take a lot to jolt Dawes off balance. "He won't be easy."

"When I hit him with this, he'll fold. I'll let you know how it comes out. Will you be at the hotel?"

Brent nodded. He took back his sack of tobacco and watched Moore move away. His sigh came from the pit of his stomach.

He didn't go out for supper. He stood at the window and watched darkness roll over town. Had Dawes suspected something and refused to come in? If so, it was going to be a tough proposition to dig him out of Broken Bit land, surrounded by Broken Bit people. Brent knew he wasn't better off as a woodchopper, but he sure didn't have all these problems.

He turned and walked to the door at the light knock on it. He opened it, and Moore slipped inside. He kicked the door shut behind him and swore in a short, bitter burst.

"Didn't Dawes come in?"

"He came in, all right. When I told him what I had on him, I thought he'd explode. He cussed me with names I never heard before." Moore squinted with pained speculation. "If he wasn't really mad, I've never seen mad before. Then he walked back to the cell and cussed Daggett and Stiles. He fired them both and said he understood now why Daggett took off so much time. He promised both of them he would blow their heads off if they ever stepped on his land again."

Brent felt a wry amusement. That was Church Dawes all right. "Was he acting?"

The pained speculation on Moore's face grew. "If he was, it was the best I ever saw. He said enough to them to rile any man regardless of what their connection was. But neither one lashed back at him. They stood and took it."

It wasn't proof, Brent thought, but it inclined a man to lean the way Moore was thinking. He was glad that Church Dawes wasn't involved, glad for Paula's sake.

"I'm going to have to turn them loose." Moore looked wild with frustration. "Two hours after Dawes left town, I got an order from the judge to release those men because of insufficient evidence. I went to see that judge. That wasn't trade whiskey Daggett was driving to the reservation. It was medicinal supplies. And all the time he talked, his honor wouldn't look at me."

"You don't think Dawes could have had everything set up?"

"I don't think he's that cute. But somebody around here is big enough to climb on that judge's back and spur him. Damn, how I want that man."

"Did you turn Daggett and Stiles loose?"

"Not yet. But I have to. I want you to pick them up when I do. See what they lead you to."

Brent nodded. He could do that. He guessed he owed Church and Paula Dawes that much.

He leaned against a wall across from the sheriff's office until he saw Daggett and Stiles come out. Moore looked after them with a morose face.

Brent moved on the opposite side of the street with the pair. They paused at the corner, said a few words, then separated.

For a moment, he was in a quandary. He couldn't follow both of them. He picked Daggett as being the more important and moved with him.

Daggett paused in the middle of a block and lit a cigarette. If he had a destination in mind, he was taking his time about getting there.

A long, slow line of cavalry, riding in pairs, turned the corner and passed between Brent and Daggett. Brent cursed them, for they blocked his sight of Daggett. He couldn't cross the street until they passed, and he swore at the leisurely pace they were taking.

When the last of them had passed. Daggett was gone. Brent

raced across the street and looked both ways. Daggett was gone. The mouth of an alley opened here, and Brent ran down it. He ran its length and saw nothing. He came back to the street and looked up and down it again. He had failed Moore on this job.

Daggett stared at that rear door. He knew who had gotten him out of jail, but he didn't know whether or not to go in and face Nader or run. He needed two things: a story Nader would accept and continuation of his job. If he didn't keep his job, he didn't keep Molly, and his guts hurt at the thought.

The truth, he thought. It would be a lot smarter than some concocted story Nader would see through immediately.

He knocked timidly on the door. One rap was all it took. The door swung open before his knuckles could touch it again.

"Get in here," Nader hissed. "I've been waiting for you."

A shiver ran through Daggett. He stepped inside, and Nader slammed the door. He shoved Daggett into the near wall with his left hand and rammed a pistol into the man's belly.

"You bastard." He was close enough so that his breath fanned Daggett's face. "I ought to kill you."

Nader's eyes were wild, and Daggett thought his breathing would stop. He managed a feeble squawk that sounded like, "Wait," and his hands rose and hung helplessly. "I didn't use your money."

"No, you stupid bastard. You went out on your own. That's almost as bad. Do you know how much it cost me to fix that judge?" He couldn't afford to let Daggett go to trial. At the moment he couldn't say what he was going to do with him. Daggett's value to him here was completely destroyed. Moore wouldn't take his eye off of him. That was another name he cursed. He had never suspected Moore was a marshal. He would have to watch every step from now on.

Daggett found a new hope. If Nader had really intended to shoot him, he wouldn't be waiting this long.

"I made a bad mistake, boss. But give me another chance."

Nader pulled the gun from Daggett's belly, and Daggett's sigh was a wheezy sound.

Nader scowled at him. "You're no good to me around here." He couldn't afford to have him running around town. He had one of two choices, hire him back or kill him. His personal choice would have been the latter. But the disposal of a body could be a risky thing. Particularly, when Moore had been alerted.

"I'll give you your job back." Nader waited until the brightness filled Daggett's face. "But not here. You can go to Whoop-up." He always needed men at Whoop-up. The monotony of life there was a grinding thing, and men drifted off or killed each other in quarrels formed out of sheer boredom.

Daggett was going to refuse. It was in his face.

Nader lifted the pistol hand again. "You really haven't much choice. That or this."

Daggett had a difficult time swallowing. "I'll go to Whoop-up."

"I thought you would. And you'll go as fast as you can get out of town."

Daggett hesitated, and Nader snapped, "What is it?"

"I'm broke. Dawes fired me, too. I haven't even got a horse."

Nader pulled some bills from is pocket and slapped them into Daggett's hand. "Don't let me catch you in town thirty minutes from now."

Daggett's profuse sweating was slowing. He had been very lucky. "You won't."

Moore hadn't blamed Brent for losing Daggett. "He's got to be in town someplace. Keep looking for him. If you pick him up again, follow him. Follow him anywhere he goes." He had given Brent a mirthless grin. "Even if he goes clear to Fort Whoop-up."

Brent had already made a pretty thorough search, and he was sure he wouldn't see Daggett again. "All right." He owed Moore the additional effort.

54

He walked down the street and said an unbelieving, "Damn."

Daggett was in almost the same spot where Brent had last seen him. He moved fast as though something chewed at his butt. It looked as though he was headed for the livery stable.

"I won't lose you this time," Brent muttered.

8

Daggett made no attempt to be devious about his trail. He left an easy-to-read track, and Brent followed him across the river and into Canada. He hadn't gone a dozen miles into Canada when he was convinced he knew where Daggett was heading. It had to be Fort Whoop-up. If so, it meant a long ride, for Whoop-up sat at the confluence of the St. Mary and Belly rivers, some two hundred and forty miles by wagon trail from Fort Benton. It would be a long and tiring ride, and Brent frowned in indecision. Moore had told him to stick with Daggett, but had he really meant for him to go as far as Whoop-up? Brent sighed and lifted the reins. Moore wanted to know where Daggett was going; he hadn't said a thing about how many miles would have to be covered.

This was the breaks, that tough, inaccessible land. There were no roads through it, and only a few trails, mostly the old game trails. A man could readly get lost here if he didn't know what he was doing. Daggett apparently knew, for his course continually bore north.

Whoop-up, all right, Brent thought. He had never seen the fort, but he had heard many stories about it. This was the second fort to sit on the site, for the original one had burned down. A freighter was supposed to have named the second one. The story went that when asked how business was, on his return to Benton for more alcohol, he had replied, "They're whooping 'em up, up there." The fort was reported to have cost twenty thousand dollars, and Brent guessed it had been set so deep in Canada to get the U. S. marshals off the traders' necks. There were three whiskey forts in Canada, but Stand-off and Slide-out didn't compare in size or volume with Whoop-up. As yet, the whiskey forts had no organized law to fear in Canada. When it came to customers, it didn't matter too much where a whiskey-trading post was built. The customers seemed to spring up out of the ground around it. Canada had large and numerous tribes. Canada was the hunting grounds of Brent's people, the Crees, and the Blackfeet and the Assiniboines were found in equally strong numbers.

He remembered his mother telling him how the Blackfeet had been named. The great fires periodically swept over the prairies, leaving mile after mile of ash-blackened earth. The Blackfeet Indians wore moccasins of white buckskin, and it didn't take many steps walking in that clinging black ash to turn those white moccasins as black as obsidian. Brent wondered who had named them, the white man or the Indian. But whichever it was, the name stuck. His face momentarily softened at the memory of that old tale.

It took most of the day to thread his way through the breaks, and Daggett's prints still headed north. He ate a semiheated can of beans and drank three cups of strong black coffee for his evening meal. Nothing showed on his face, but his mouth and throat protested at the taste of the coffee. He had never made a decent cup of coffee in his life.

His eye had a moody reflectiveness as he went back over the past few weeks. Things had changed for him in a hurry since the moment Moore had slugged him on the jaw, for better and worse. Certainly, better materially. But not better mentally. For his loneliness had increased. Even now the picture of a face was trying to form in the flames of the campfire. He suspected that that face would always be around to haunt him. Most of a man's life was futility. Knowing Paula was in that class.

"One wrong move, and you're dead." The voice came from the blackness beyond the range of the firelight.

The unexpectedness of it momentarily froze Brent's mind, then he cursed himself. He had been walking in the quicksand of his thoughts, and he hadn't been alert to anything else. His rifle was propped up on his saddle a dozen yards away, and he kept his hand a careful distance from the butt

56

of his pistol. He hadn't identified the voice from those few words, but it had a familiar ring. He cursed himself again. The very least that could happen to him was that he'd be stripped of all his possessions and left afoot. If he made it back to Fort Benton, what would he do then? Walk up to Moore and confess another failure?

"Unbuckle the belt."

Brent carefully obeyed. He almost had the voice that time. Daggett? The name popped into his mind. If so, the man had doubled back and caught Brent while his mind was asleep.

Daggett stepped into the radius of the firelight, and the rifle muzzle never wavered from Brent's chest. Brent didn't know whether or not seeing Daggett was a reason for relief. He had never been a favorite of Daggett's while he worked for Church Dawes. He had to take this a slow, cautious step at a time until he saw where it led. A jeering inner voice asked him, And if Daggett decides to take everything you have, what are you going to do about it?

Right at the moment not a damned thing, Brent admitted to the voice.

Daggett's eyes were mean in a cold-set face. "Why were you following me?"

Brent threw out his hands. "I wasn't following you."

"The hell you weren't. Do you think I'm blind? Every time I hit a high point and looked back, there you were. Why you lying Indian sonuvabitch"—Brent felt the involuntary twitching of his flesh. The moment trembled on a razor's edge, and Daggett's rage could put the necessary pull into his trigger finger—"who sent you after me?"

Brent shook his head. "I didn't know you were anywhere around. Dawes fired me. I couldn't find work around Benton. I was heading home to my people, the Crees."

Daggett mulled that over, and some of the rage faded from his face.

The moment still teetered, but Brent dared to draw a longer breath. Dawes had fired Daggett, too, and the man had no reason to be fond of him. Brent had had no time to think of a better reason, and maybe the truth served him best.

"Why did he fire you?"

"His daughter—" Brent let the rest of it go into a shrug.

57

It must have carried conviction, for a brief grin touched Daggett's face. "You were sweet on her? Why, you damn fool. You're lucky he didn't blow your head off." He laughed harshly. "I wish I could've seen the old bastard's face when he found out about it."

Brent allowed himself a small sigh. Their common dislike of Dawes fashioned a small bond between them. "He knocked me down and threw me off his place. Someday I'll see him again and—" He let the rest of the threat die.

The rifle muzzle strayed a small fraction from its steady pointing. Daggett's face twisted in sudden malevolence. "You'll have to stand in line after me." He debated something with himself. "Do you know this country? Are there Indians around?"

"This is Cree country. I thought I'd see some of them before now." The tightness in Brent's chest was melting rapidly as he guessed at what was in Daggett's mind.

"Do they know you?"

"A lot of them." That was a lie. He hadn't seen the Crees in years.

"Maybe we could ride together. You could say we're friends."

Brent nodded solemnly. "In this country it is always safer for two men than one."

Daggett grounded the rifle butt. His eyes narrowed with sudden suspicion. "If you try to cross me—"

"Why should I? You never treated me bad on Dawes' place."

Now the relief was on Daggett's face. "That's so, isn't it? Any of that coffee left?"

He stepped to the fire without waiting for Brent's reply and poured the remaining coffee into a cup. He spat it out after a taste. "My God! Do you call that coffee?"

Brent grinned. "I'm known for my bad coffee."

"Pack up your stuff and move to my camp. I'll make you a decent cup."

Brent smiled to himself as he packed. This couldn't have gone better if he had had a choice. Daggett hadn't said where he was going, but it didn't matter. This would be so much easier than having to trail him. He wasn't particularly desirous of Daggett's company, but he would take it a thousand times over the moment he had faced just a few minutes ago.

They rode for two days, always north, and Daggett grew more talkative, particularly around the campfires. He talked a great deal about Molly Sanders. Brent knew her by sight. She was a brassy, painted blonde with a loud, aggressive laugh. He didn't see how she could appeal to any man, but Daggett made it plain how he felt about her. Brent hid his grimace. He didn't think Daggett would spend much time at Whoop-up. Molly Sanders would pull him back.

His eyes caught the glimmer of firelight far ahead in the gathering darkness. He pointed it out to Daggett, and Daggett asked, "Indians?"

Brent shook his head, and there was contempt in the gesture. Indians wouldn't build a fire so openly or carelessly. That fire could be seen for miles in any direction on this open prairie.

"It could be freighters," Daggett muttered. "Let's go see."

Brent was afraid Daggett would ride openly into the camp, but Daggett was wiser than that. He ordered the horses left a good distance from the camp, and they worked a cautious way to it. Four men sat around the fire, and Brent thought, My God, how can men be so careless? They didn't even have a guard out, and the wagons and two teams half hidden in shadow, were more than enough invitation to any wandering band of Indians.

Brent felt the tenseness flow out of Daggett. "I know two of them," he said. "Preston and Mitchell. Independent whiskey traders. They probably picked up the other two as helpers."

"They're taking a hell of a chance."

Daggett grinned. "They'll wake up dead some morning. But for the profits, they'll risk it. It happens to a lot of the independents."

Brent grunted. A white man risked a lot for profits. He wished what Daggett forecast for Preston and Mitchell would happen to all the whiskey traders.

Daggett straightened. "It's okay to go on in. Maybe we'll stay the night and eat off them." He looked impatiently at Brent. "Come on. I said I knew them."

Brent looked uneasily about him. The darkness prevented him from seeing anything, but his skin crawled with some premonition. He reluctantly followed Daggett.

One of the four men made a bound for his rifle, and Preston yelled, "It's okay. I know Daggett."

He pumped Daggett's hand. He was a big, bearded man in filthy clothes. Brent was downwind of him, and he moved a few paces. The man reeked.

Mitchell grinned at Daggett. "You lost, Daggett?"

"I'm on my way to Whoop-up." Daggett threw a quick look at Brent. If Brent heard that, he didn't show it, or it didn't make any difference to him. "You came in pretty far, didn't you?"

It was no source of worry to either of them. "We've got twelve rifles along," Mitchell said. "How many Indians are going to face those?"

Daggett introduced Brent, and they looked curiously at him. Apparently they saw his Indian blood, for the question was big in their eyes.

"He's just riding with me." Daggett offered no other explanation, and they accepted it.

Preston spat at the ground. "You're just in time. We're mixing up a batch. A couple of Assiniboines came by this afternoon. They're bringing in the tribe tomorrow."

The four men were cast in the same pattern: big, bearded, and dirty. A casual glance wouldn't have picked out one from the other.

Daggett shook his head. "I can't help you any."

Preston laughed. "Don't give me that. With as much of the stuff as you've mixed. You can at least taste it, can't you? and tell me if it's all right."

The wagon bed was half filled with tins of raw alcohol. One of the helpers poked holes in two tins and dumped them into a huge pot. The reek of raw alcohol was overpowering.

Daggett whispered to Brent. "A gallon of raw alcohol to more than three gallons of water. They're cutting the alcohol short. The Indians won't be happy about that. That's tea they're putting in now. A pound of it to a gallon of alcohol for flavor and color. Now some rank black chewing-tobacco for more flavor. Add some Jamaica ginger and a handful of red peppers. Injun whiskey should take the top of a man's head off. If I was handling it, I'd add some black molasses. The northern tribes are used to Hudson Bay rum, and they like the taste. But Preston and Mitchell won't spend a penny that isn't necessary."

Brent moodily watched the mixing. Most of the tribes called this foul mixture firewater. The Crees had another name for it, perhaps more realistic. They called it *iskota-wapoo*, or fire liquid.

Preston dipped out a cupful and handed it to Daggett. Daggett tasted it. "Little weak, isn't it?"

Preston grinned. "It goes farther that way."

All four men were busy filling the pint containers. The standard rate of exchange was a pint for a buffalo robe, a robe worth five dollars in Benton.

"Get one swallow down an Indian, and he can't stop himself," Daggett said. "He'll trade everything he's got for more, including his squaw and daughters. By the time they get this wagonload traded, they'll make around two thousand dollars."

He tried another taste. "This is pretty bad. It's traders like these that keep the quality going down. But the Indian doesn't care. He'll drink anything." He handed the cup to Brent. "This'll make a man out of you."

Brent had tasted trade whiskey before. As far as he was concerned, he had had enough of it to last him a lifetime.

Mild surprise washed Daggett's face as Brent made no move to take the cup. "Hell, I thought all Indians were crazy about—"

He broke off under those cold, stabbing eyes. "You know what I mean," he finished lamely.

"I know what you mean." Brent walked away. He looked back, and tin cups were passing from hand to hand. Brent's stomach had a memory, too, for it lurched in a queasy convulsion. He wondered how much of the stuff they would drink. He shrugged the question away. It was their heads and stomachs. He picked up his bedroll and melted away into the darkness. Maybe he was being overly cautious, but he was going to sleep a good distance from this camp. He hoped it wouldn't happen, but he had no intentions of helping to defend the camp if it was attacked.

61

He found a hollow that fitted his hips and pulled his blanket up around him. Faint snatches of loud laughter drifted to him. Maybe he hadn't moved far enough away. He was still thinking about it when he fell asleep.

9

HE WASN'T sure that wasn't disappointment he felt in the morning when he found the camp intact.

Daggett glowered at him when he came in. "Where in the hell did you fade to last night?"

Brent jerked his head toward the prairie. "I slept out there. I knew if I was going to get any sleep, it wouldn't be here."

Daggett gave him an edgy grin. "You showed more smart than I did. I drank too much of that damned rotgut."

His complexion showed it, and his hand wasn't quite steady as he reached for the coffeepot. "There's more coffee. If you want anything else, fix it yourself."

Coffee would do, Brent decided. Maybe Daggett would feel more like eating a little later. "When are we moving on?"

Daggett groaned. "The way my head feels, never. It won't hurt to stick around a little while." He nodded toward the four blanketed forms. "Maybe seeing them wake up suffering will help mine."

With the coming of light the crawling on Brent's skin had stopped, but he still would have liked to be a long way from here. Maybe he was a trouble borrower, but something told him the course of wisdom led away from here as fast as possible.

The first of the Assiniboines came in an hour later, his face eager with anticipation. He spoke no English, but the proffered robe needed no explanation.

Preston had just awakened, and he was in a foul mood. "Get out of here. Let me get my legs under me."

The eager smile remained on the Indian's face, and he kept holding out the robe.

"I'll bend a gun barrel over his head. Maybe he'll understand that." Preston's eyes went to Brent. "Can you talk to him?"

"Maybe a little."

"Then tell him noon. Not ready until noon." He strode away, and the Indian's smile slowly faded.

His face lengthened as Brent told him, no trading until noon. Preston probably hadn't planned things that way, but it was a subtle cruelty to make the man wait.

The Assiniboines had camped two hundred yards from the whiskey camp, and Brent walked there with this Indian. The man's normal reticence vanished when he learned Brent was half Cree. The Assiniboines and Crees were at peace right now.

The Indian waved his hand at the dozen tipis. "Much trade," he said happily.

It was an unusually small camp, and Brent doubted this was all of them. Where were the others? The answer to that could be damned important.

This Assiniboine looked carefree enough, but Brent thought there was too much watchfulness in the covert glances he kept putting on him.

Brent tried to talk to the squaws, and they looked at him stolid-faced without responding. He noticed one of them slipping away from the tipis, her arms laden with guns and knives. He remembered a white man describing a scene of getting drunk with Indians. "The first thing the squaws do," the man had said, "is to cache the guns and knives. That's to keep the braves from killing each other. That was the first time I ever tried that trade whiskey. A dozen of us were on a trail drive, and we ran into these Indians on the banks of the Missouri. A few drinks of that trade whiskey made the Missouri look like a creek, and we rode into it with no fear. That stuff was sure a brave-maker, and if a man had enough of it in him, he couldn't drown. Hell, I swear to you, if a man had been drinking that stuff, you could shoot him through the brain or heart, and he wouldn't die till he sobered up. When Indians get their hides full, they're bad and dangerous. We all got drunk together, and inside an hour all of us were so disagreeable, we couldn't stand each other. Then the fighting started. We were smart enough to leave our guns at camp, and an Indian ain't worth a damn when it comes to using his fists. About all he can do is to pull hair, and with him wearing his hair long, we had the advantage. We got so mean, the Indians couldn't stand us and pulled up stakes and left us."

Brent grinned sourly as he remembered the roar of laughter that went up when the man finished the narration. But the thread of worry remained. He still wished he knew if there were other Assiniboines around.

Near noon Preston fired a pistol into the air, and the Indians rushed the whiskey camp. They snatched up the pints of whiskey, and the pile of robes grew. Preston wouldn't let them drink in the camp. He waved them away, and when they had something else to trade, they could return.

The trading went on through the afternoon, and the success of it put the traders in high spirits. Brent noticed all of them were taking an occasional belt, and by nightfall they were lurching as they moved. The Indians ran out of robes and offered furs. When those were gone, they brought in their weapons. Most of them were old muskets, and the traders contemptuously rejected them. Daggett was getting as drunk as the rest of them, and Brent thought, You damned fool. Wasn't last night enough?

The traders still had whiskey left, but the trade was slowing down. The Indians brought in mostly junk now, and only occasionally did the traders pick up an item that had any value. If they were smart, they would pack up and get out of here as fast as they could. But their brains had been watered down by the whiskey. It would take hours of sleep to wear off this drunk.

Brent melted away from the camp. Fires burned between the Indian lodges, and he saw leaping, dancing figures silhouetted against the flames. Several of the Indians had already fallen into unconsciousness, and it wouldn't take long to put the rest on the ground beside the motionless forms. That crawling was starting on his skin again. Something that wasn't peaceful was abroad in the air, and it had a clammy touch. He didn't feel it came from the Indian camp, but it was out there somewhere.

He moved through the dark night on foot, making his casts in wider circles about the camp. He told himself he was foolish, but something drove him on.

He froze as the night breeze carried the faint sound to him, the stomping of a horse.

He crept up as closely as he dared, and there in the bottom of a gulch he found the missing braves. There must have been better than twenty shadowy figures below him, a few of them mounted, the rest hunkered down and engaged in low conversation.

He was as silent as a snake, slithering back from that edge, and his breathing was painfully tight. He knew what those Indians were waiting for; they were waiting for the traders to become so drunk that the deadly rifles were no longer effective. He shivered as he thought that the waiting time must be nearly over.

Nobody paid any attention to him when he returned to camp. The traders were still on their feet but staggering now Daggett leaned against a wagon wheel, a fixed grin on his face. You damned fools, Brent thought.

He slipped his and Daggett's horses away from the camp and picketed them out on the prairie. He carried saddles and gear to them, and though the chilly night breeze wrapped around him, he was sweating. Every passing minute cut cruelly into whatever margin of time he had left.

He had been sure he wasn't going to open his mouth to Preston or Mitchell, but he had to say something.

Preston's eyes were glassy and wandering, and Brent had trouble making him listen. "Get out of here," he said urgently. "I found a war party waiting to ride in on you."

Preston stared at him, and Brent took hold of his arm "Don't you understand? I found—"

Preston flung his arm, shaking off Brent's grip. "You goddamned liar. You haven't been out of camp all evening." His eyes narrowed suspiciously "Why, you damned Indian What are you planning?"

He threw a wild punch that Brent blocked with an upflung arm. He shoved the man, and Preston went down hard. He was drunker than Brent thought, for he glared about him, trying to place Brent. He struggled to get back on his feet, and Brent didn't wait to see whether or not he was successful. He got away from there as fast as he could. Preston would be grabbing for his gun next.

He put Preston out of his mind. He had done all he could for him; he had tried.

He found Daggett and took his arm. "I want to show you something."

Daggett was in an amiable mood, and he came willingly. Brent led him beyond the reach of the firelight, and a little argument crept into Daggett's voice. "Where the hell are we going?"

"Just a couple steps more." The horses were some fifty yards ahead, and Daggett was a big man. Brent didn't want to drag him any farther than he had to.

He got a dozen more steps out of him before Daggett stopped, suspicion in every line of him. "Just what the hell are you trying to pull on me?"

Brent stepped in close. He hit the bottom half of that pale oval before him. The hard impact ran the length of this arm, and for a half-blind punch, it was a good one. He caught Daggett full on the jaw point, tearing a garbled sound out of him. He was ready to hit him again, but he didn't have to. Daggett swayed and plunged forward on his face. Brent bent over him. Daggett was out cold.

He put his hands under the armpits and dragged him toward the horses, cursing that heavy inert weight every foot of the way. He was bathed in sweat by the time he reached them. If Daggett's horse shied on him, he was going to kick its damned head off. He would have enough trouble as it was getting Daggett across his saddle.

The horse turned its head and looked at him, but it didn't shy. He had a hell of a time getting Daggett on his feet. The man was all flopping arms and legs. He managed to get his shoulder under Daggett's breastbone and lifted him with a mighty heave. Daggett started spilling to one side, and Brent grabbed wildly to steady him. He thought he was going to lose him, and his lungs heaved under the effort. He put all of his strength into the final lift. He got Daggett up and partially across the saddle. The horse snorted, and Brent thought, I'll kill you if you move now. He pushed on Daggett and slid him forward until he was draped across the saddle. Daggett hung there, arms and legs dangling.

It hadn't taken more than a few seconds, but Brent was drained. He gasped in air until the trembling left his muscles.

He thought about tying him in place, but a sense of urgency was pushing him. Daggett should ride the way he was.

Brent led both horses, moving slowly. He hadn't gone a hundred yards when he heard the rattling of rifle fire. He shivered as the wild yelling drifted to him. That margin had been cut thin, too thin. After that first sporadic burst of gunfire, the silence fell, heavy and oppressive. Preston and the others had been in no condition to put up much of a defense.

He kept up that steady walking until he judged he had covered better than a mile. He found a small coulee and led the horses into it.

He pushed on Daggett and dumped him to the ground, not worrying about his fall. He led the horses a little farther down the coulee and picketed them. He came back and turned Daggett over on his back. Daggett snored in stentorian blasts. He hadn't felt a thing.

Brent spent a long, strained night. Toward morning he dozed in fitful snatches. When the light strengthened, he tried to awaken Daggett and could get no response out of him. Maybe it would be best to let him sleep it out. He was sure Daggett was going to be in a quarrelsome mood when he awakened.

The sun climbed higher, driving the chill from the air and drying the dew.

Daggett muttered and turned over, shielding his face from the heat of the sun. Brent tried again to arouse him, but the wall of unconsciousness was too thick to get through.

An hour later Daggett stirred and groaned. Brent sat on his heels, watching him. Daggett fought coming out of his pit. He made incoherent sounds and flung his arms. It took a good fifteen minutes for him to get his eyes open. He closed them immediately, groaning as the sunlight blasted into his skull.

Brent felt no pity for his suffering. Daggett had earned every minute of it.

Daggett opened his eyes again and stared vacantly about him. His cheeks looked hollow, showing the stamp of last night. His eyes touched first one object, then another, without understanding. At last they fastened on Brent, and some emotion twisted his face.

He heaved himself into a sitting position, and the effort was costly. It showed in the groan that slipped out of him, in the sudden contorting of his face.

He sat with head bent between his knees before he cautiously raised it. He felt of his jaw, and it must have been tender because of the gentle fingering of it. He looked at Brent, and his eyes were ugly. Things were slowly coming back to him.

"Why goddam you. You hit me."

Brent nodded. "Don't reach for your gun. I've got it."

That was a wise precaution, for if ever a man wanted to kill another, Daggett did.

Brent listened impassively to Daggett cursing him. "You'll be thanking me in a little while. I got you out just before an Indian attack on Preston's camp."

Daggett called him a liar in every way he knew.

Brent's patience snapped. "Come on. I'll show you."

He had to help Daggett to his feet, had to help him into his saddle. Daggett slumped there, a sick man.

Brent walked the horses back to camp, keeping a sharp lookout, though he thought the Indians would be long gone.

A heavy, brooding silence hung over the campsite, but it no longer looked like a camp. The teams were gone, and the wagon had been burned. Pint bottles were strewn all over the place. He looked toward the Indian camp. The lodges were gone. The Indians had had quite a night for themselves. They had their trade goods back and the whiskey, too.

He looked once at the four bodies, then wrenched his eyes from them. They had been horribly mutilated, and the tops of their heads were raw, the red oozing just now crusting over.

He glanced at Daggett. Daggett was erect in his saddle, his face a ghastly white.

"I did some scouting last night." Brent's voice was matter-of-fact. "There was a bunch of them, waiting to come in when the traders were drunk enough. I led the horses away, then came back and got you."

"My God!" Daggett's small, wheezing voice barely managed to carry the words. He couldn't take his eyes from the sad corpses. "My God. You saved my life." His eyes swung to Brent, and they asked the question, Why?

Brent shrugged. "We were riding together. I tried to warn Preston. He wouldn't listen to me."

A single thought seemed to be in Daggett's head. "You saved me." He wrestled with it for a moment, then added, "Are you still looking for a job?"

Elation leaped within Brent. He wished Moore knew about this. This wasn't failure.

"I'd take one."

"I'm going to Fort Whoop-up. I can promise you a job there."

Brent appeared to consider it. "Why not?"

That was real warmth in Daggett's grin. "I was a lucky man to run into you."

Maybe, Brent thought. Maybe not.

They rode away without a backward glance. Without a shovel they couldn't do much for those four. Brent thought about it for a moment then pushed it out of his head. It wouldn't matter much to them anyway.

10

THEY TOPPED a small rise, and Daggett waved a hand before him. "There she is. Fort Whoop-up. It cost twenty thousand dollars to build and cheap at four times the price."

Brent stared at the infamous trading post. Moore would give anything to be able to smash it. A frown rode Brent's face. Even if Moore had been here, what could he have done about it? That brought up another worry. How was he even going to let Moore know where he was?

Daggett gloomily shook his head. "A whole goddamned summer, at least, spent in this hole. We might as well go on in."

Brent wasn't easy of spirit as they rode toward it. The post was a hollow square stockade with walls of tightly joined logs, set vertically about fourteen feet high. The upright posts sharpened on the ends, and he guessed this was to keep the Indians from climbing over the walls.

Daggett nodded as though Brent had asked a question. "I've seen times when a man's damned grateful for those walls. When an Indian gets drunk, he tries to scramble over them after more whiskey. The sharpened ends make it harder. We've got a walkway near the top where a man can stand and push them off with long poles." His grin flashed at some memory. "They fall pretty damned hard."

They were seen coming, for a thick oaken gate swung open to admit them. It contained a small wicket, and Brent wondered about its purpose.

A dozen men were on hand to greet them, and many of them knew Daggett. They hailed him with ribald greetings and put a cold curiosity on Brent. He had never seen a tougher-looking bunch of men. All of them were heavily armed, most of them with a brace of pistols, and many a boot top contained a sheathed knife. He wondered sourly if they knew what that stuff flowing in the two rivers was. By their appearances they didn't believe it had anything to do with washing.

The bastions at the corners of the stockade were loopholed for rifles. Brent saw a small cannon and a mountain howitzer mounted so that they commanded a wide sweep of the prairie. A large log building was built against one inside wall and partitioned off into rooms for dwellings, blacksmith shop, and stores. The doors, windows, and even chimney openings were barred with iron strips to prevent entry by drunken Indians in the event they ever got inside the stockade.

A foul smell hung over the post. The reek of raw alcohol was predominant, and Brent imagined they had recently mixed up a large batch of trade whiskey. The men's clothes were permeated with the smell, and he knew that wasn't the first batch that had gone into the garments. As offensive as that part of the stench was, it was mild compared with the rest of its component parts. A million flies buzzed over a garbage heap, and he saw animal offal, hides, and heads thrown upon it. The flies rose angrily into the air as the men passed the heap, then settled back.

Brent silently echoed Daggett's plaint. It was going to be hell cooped up in this place for any length of time.

"Where's Hampton?" Daggett asked one of the men.

The man jerked his thumb toward the blacksmith, and his eyes returned to Brent. Brent was well aware of the cold, measuring quality in them.

He heard the ring of hammer against metal coming from the building as he dismounted. Daggett waited for a lull in the hammering, then bellowed, "Hey, Hampton. Come out here."

Hampton waddled out of the door. He was a man big of frame but gone to lard. His belly flopped over his belt and shook as he moved. He had a pockmarked face and small eyes that kept shifting constantly.

Daggett grinned mockingly at him. "Hog, this is Brent Bargen. The boss said put him to work."

Brent knew a stab of disappointment. He had hoped that Dagget would say a name.

He saw the flash of naked hatred in Hampton's face. It left no doubt as to how he felt about Daggett.

Hampton thrust out a meaty hand, and Brent took it. The outer softness built up a wrong impression. There was surprising strength beneath that softness.

"Hoge Hampton," he said. "Daggett thinks he's a very funny man. Someday he might get smart enough to learn how to pronounce my name."

Daggett spat between his feet. "Horse shit."

Brent watched them covertly. The animosity between them was of long standing and deep planted. That kind of planting always produced violence. A man could figure on it as surely as there would be a tomorrow.

Hampton's eyes rested on Daggett with a heavy calculation. "What did he send you up here for?"

"To see what's going wrong. He wasn't happy about your last report."

Rage washed Hampton's face. "Then tell him to put more protection on his supply trains. The last one didn't get through at all."

"Should I tell him you're not happy about the way he's running things?" Daggett enjoyed his baiting of Hampton. "What would you suggest? That he go to the army and ask it to guard his supply trains for him?"

Again that lightning flash of hating was in Hampton's eyes.

He was, no doubt, a little slow-witted, and he couldn't keep up with Daggett's more facile mind and tongue. When he was pushed too far, he would turn to something else, something that would make a wound that would hurt a hell of a lot more than a cleverly turned phrase. Brent knew that if Hampton were his enemy, he would hate to go to sleep around him.

Hampton took Brent's arm. "Come on. I'll show you around."

Daggett made no attempt to follow them, but he called, "Don't worry, Hog. I'll be around for a while. We'll have plenty of time for our talks."

Hampton quivered with rage. He was as heavy-footed as a draft animal, and he plowed straight through to the question that troubled him. "Why was he sent up here? To replace me?"

Brent started to say that he knew nothing of Daggett's background, that he had met him on the trail, and he stopped the words just in time. That wouldn't be smart at all, to destroy the identity Daggett had given him.

"I don't know." He didn't have to pretend to be honest about that.

Hampton gave him a long, searching scrutiny. His sigh said that he was satisfied and disappointed, too. "I guess you wouldn't," he muttered.

He walked along for several yards in silence. "Are you new in this business?"

The unexpectedness of the question startled Brent. "My first try at it."

"Do you know what it is?" Hampton put a frowning intentness on him.

"I know. I've seen a little of it. But a man takes what he can get. I'm a breed." He used the word apparently without feeling. "We don't get a choice of jobs."

"Ah." Hampton seemed lost in thought. Evidently he decided he could win this man to him. "I wondered about your looks. The others might try to make it rough on you. I'll keep them off you all I can."

"Thanks." The word was emotionless.

Hampton was struggling with some load that he had to spill over. "It's a rotten, filthy business. Most of us have reasons like yours for going into it." He smiled faintly. "It's

72

hard to believe that I was once a respected businessman in Benton. But I couldn't stay away from the gaming tables." His hands moved in a vague gesture. "I turned all my old friends against me by constant begging for money. Maybe I was like you. With the hold gambling had on me, I didn't have much of a choice."

Brent put a hard hand on any shoot of pity that might sprint up for Hampton. The man had had a choice. He chose this.

Hampton's face twisted. "You wouldn't believe the class of men I get up here. They have to be unprincipled blackguards to engage in this brutal business. But they have no fear. Many of them are Civil War veterans, or graduates of the bushwhacker or outlaw gangs that roamed Missouri and Kansas." He pointed to the flag flying on a staff over one of the bastions. "The American flag. Flying on Canadian soil. No wonder the Indian mind associates it with drunken debauchery, fraud and cruelty. There's no law around here except that of self-preservation. The Indians flock here to get the whiskey, but they know what we're doing to them. They shoot whiskey traders on sight if they can catch them alone on the plains." He smiled bleakly. "Remember that. Watch every step when you leave these walls. You won't be safe outside, and you won't be safe here. It tells on a man's nerves after a while. Quarrels come easy. If one arises, don't try to talk your way out of it. Shoot him before he shoots you."

Brent listened soberly. This sounded like a well-educated man. Every day he spent here must be torture to him. If he had to make a choice between Hampton and Daggett, it would be an easy one.

A tinge of malice was in Hampton's smile. "Do I make it sound attractive enough? The Indians and the whiskey traders aren't your worst enemies. Those are the wolfers, the toughest men I ever saw. They live by pelting wolves. They poison the buffalo carcasses as bait for the wolves. But the Indians' dogs get at the poison and die. Then some of the Indians do, for they eat the dogs. The Indians hate the wolfers. I've seen wolfers so stuck with arrows they look like a pincushion. The wolfers hate us because we'll trade the Indians repeating rifles and modern ammunition. It makes it easier for the Indians to pick them off at long range. The

73

wolfer will kill a whiskey trader as quick as any Indian would. It makes for a peaceful life. Do you still think you want to work here?"

No, Brent didn't want to work here. He put a strained grin on his face. "I haven't changed my mind."

"It's your skin. I'll show you where you sleep."

Hampton led the way to a small room inside the large log building. It was a bare little room, holding a cot and a chair. The floor was mud caked, and the smell that hung over the fort had permeated this room.

Hampton's eyes were amused as he watched Brent look about the room. "Home. Do you need help bringing your stuff in?"

Brent shook his head. He didn't have that much. He thought Hampton would leave him, but the man lingered. He suddenly discovered the answer. Hampton was lonely. His question confirmed it. "Would you like to look over the post?"

Brent nodded and followed him out of the door. Hampton's speech proved he was a far cut above the others, and Brent imagined he associated with the men here as little as possible. Perhaps Hampton thought he had found somebody to talk to. In its way it was a compliment.

Hampton gave him a thorough tour of the post. The last stop was the powder room. It was well stocked. One wall was lined with kegs of powder, and one of them, sitting on the floor, had its head knocked in. Hampton pointed out the opened keg. "We do a good business in trading powder. Most of the Indians have old muskets."

He waited for Brent to leave the room, then pulled the door to behind him.

Brent had noticed the rifles and boxes of cartridges in the room. With that arsenal the post could hold off half the Indians in Canada.

Brent's face was thoughtful. "It's quite a layout."

"It's a money-making thing. But he's never satisfied."

Brent caught the bitterness in Hampton's voice. By "he" he must mean the man behind this. Brent wished he had that name.

They passed within a dozen yards of Daggett, and Brent

didn't miss the scowl on his face. Daggett didn't like the time Hampton was spending with Brent.

"You and Daggett don't seem to care for each other."

"That son-of-a-bitch." The words exploded from Hampton. "We had a clash in Fort Benton. He's never forgotten it. I'll have to kill him before it's over."

Brent wondered if he could. From surface appearances he would say not. He could be caught right in the middle of their argument, for both men seemed to be trying to put some kind of claim on him.

Hampton changed the subject. "You got here just in time. The Blackfeet come in tomorrow to trade. If you've never seen it before, it'll be quite a day."

Brent didn't comment. He had seen it. The picture of four mutilated bodies flashed into his mind. But that wasn't likely to happen here.

A man came out of a doorway and bumped squarely into him. The impact put Brent back a staggering step. He caught his balance, and his tone was sharp. "Watch where you're going."

The man was short and squatty and rolling drunk. A livid scar bisected the part of his cheek his beard didn't hide. Red eyes glared at Brent. "Why, you sonuvabitch. You bumped into me."

Brent suspected he was naturally quarrelsome, and the liquor hadn't helped it any. The scene had already attracted attention. If he took a backward step, he was through before he got started.

"That's enough, Mace," Hampton said. "There's no harm done."

"That ain't my opinion." Mace's hand hardly appeared to move, and there was a knife in it. "I'll cut on him a little and improve his manners."

Brent fell back another step, his eyes narrowed and watchful. "There's no need for that."

Mace moved toward him in mincing steps, the knife blade flashing in circles. He jumped at Brent, the knife tip darting forward, and laughed as Brent took a hasty backward step. "You afraid, Indian?" He shoved the blade forward again, delighting in the jerking of Brent's facial muscles.

"I'm going to learn you something, Indian. I'm going to learn it to you real well."

"Mace," Hampton yelled again.

Mace snarled at him without turning his head. Nothing was going to stop him.

Brent's hand moved closer to the pistol butt. Mace was readying for a leap toward him. The moment he started it—The thought shattered as Mace yelled and jumped. Brent drew the gun. Maybe he had cut it a little fine. His thought was to hit the man in the shoulder, but there wasn't time for a fine aim. He had to hit Mace wherever he could.

He fired at the end of the draw. The slug smashed into Mace's chest and slammed him back a couple of steps. His head lifted out of his crouch, and shock and surprise made his face rigid. The knife fell from his hand, puffing up a little cloud of dust. He took a staggered step, his foot slamming down hard. The stain in the center of his chest spread rapidly. He looked at Brent with some kind of desperate appeal in his eyes, then plunged forward into the dirt.

Brent shook inwardly. It had happened too suddenly, and it was so damned unnecessary. He held the pistol as he swung his eyes around the small circle of watching men. "Does anybody want a part of this?" He didn't know how many friends Mace might have had.

They stared back at him with calculating eyes. Several of them shook their heads. Only one of them spoke. "The least little thing always set Mace off. I guess he asked for it."

A nod ran around the circle. That seemed to be the consensus.

"Take him away," Hampton ordered. He waited until four men picked up Mace and carried him away. Maybe he sensed a sickness behind Brent's eyes. "Nobody's blaming you. This could work out well for you. You made your stand and backed it up."

All Brent wanted to do was to get away from them, but he wouldn't let a too-hasty departure trip him up. Daggett was watching him with a speculative scowl on his face.

"Welcome to Fort Whoop-up," Hampton said, and pulled Brent's attention back to him.

11

DAGGETT CAME into his room after dark. Brent was lying down, and Daggett took the chair. "They're talking about you."

Brent kept staring at the ceiling. "I didn't want to kill him."

"It's bothering you, huh?" Daggett laughed. "Mace was about through here. If you hadn't done it, somebody else would. It puts you off on the right foot. The boys are saying you're pretty fast."

Hampton had told Brent much the same thing, and it eased nothing. Why hadn't he done what he had wanted to and given the badge back to Moore?

Daggett's voice hardened. "You spent a lot of time with Hampton. You figure on it doing you some good?"

Brent turned his head toward him. "I never even thought of that."

"Don't. If you want to pick somebody to cozy up to, you pick me. Hampton won't last long."

They locked hard eyes, and Daggett laughed as he got to his feet. "Remember what I said. It could be bad if you picked the wrong man."

He sauntered to the door, turned there, and put another long, hard look on Brent.

Brent swore softly as the door closed. He was right in thinking those two would be tugging at him. It left him a narrow line to walk without offending either of them. He locked his hands behind his head and resumed staring at the ceiling. He wasn't looking forward to tomorrow; he wasn't looking forward to any day he had to stay here. Give me a name, he thought in sudden desperation. That's all I need.

He stood at the gate with Hampton in the morning and watched the band of Blackfeet draw nearer. They stopped some four hundred yards from the post, and the squaws began setting up the lodges.

"The braves are getting painted up." Hampton squinted at

the rising lodges. "I'd guess about fifty lodges. As good as I hoped for. I hope they brought plenty of pemmican with them. We're about out. That's what this post lives on." He made a wry face. "It's not bad. If a man's hungry enough." He stared toward the Indian encampment. "Ah, they're coming. They made quick time of their painting. They must be eager."

Forty or fifty braves on horseback dashed toward the post. They rode at breakneck speed, brandishing rifles and ancient muskets. They were hideously painted, and it looked like a war party to Brent, yet Hampton showed no alarm. He must have sensed Brent's disquiet, for he grinned. "There's a careful routine handed down by experience. They're only demonstrating their willingness to trade. First, they'll stage a dance before the gate, then we'll let in a few of the leaders."

Brent's eyes were on the rapidly approaching party. Maybe so, he thought dubiously. But he noticed that the oak gate hadn't swung open.

The Indians threw off their ponies, and the din of their shrill voices pounded at a man's eardrums. They went into the dance with much savage stomping that drove their heels against the earth. Their greased bodies bent like bows, then snapped erect. It was a ferocious and perhaps a frightening thing to watch.

It went on until chests were heaving and mouths were open, gasping for breath; then suddenly it was over. Six of the Indians broke off from the main body and approached the gate.

Hampton moved forward to greet them, and Brent stayed close to him. If he was curious about anything, he had found the man willing and even anxious to answer questions.

The gate opened to admit the six, and the greeting between Indian and white man was a solemn thing, filled with dignity and mutual flattery. The Indians were given a free drink, and their hands trembled with eagerness as they reached for it.

They gulped it down, and Brent saw the constriction of their faces as the potent liquor bit at them. One chief said, "Wah," and they looked at each other, smacking their lips and nodding with approval.

Outside the closed gate the remaining Indians capered with

impatience for the ceremony of greeting to end. The leaders, inside the post, politely extended their cups for another drink, and Brent was surprised to see whiskey poured into them. How many free drinks did a trading post give?

The Indians held the searing liquid in their mouths as they jumped to their feet. They ran toward the gate, and it swung open before them. They spat the liquor into the eagerly opened mouths of their friends, then all of them ran for their horses. They raised a thick cloud of dust as they raced for their camp.

"They will be back with goods to trade," Hampton said. "We used to include the Hudson Bay Company's regale in the opening ceremony. That's the giving of a free drink all around. But we found it too time-consuming and expensive." He shrugged. "And not necessary. It opened as a tame day, didn't it? But it's not over yet. You'll earn your pay."

He yelled an order to several men to, "get that damned gate closed and barred" and stationed himself at the wicket.

The Indians returned with ponies burdened with buffalo robes, furs, and buffalo-hide sacks of pemmican. They fought to be first in line before the wicket. Brent wouldn't have believed Hampton could move this swiftly. He took in the trade goods through the wicket and handed back the bottles of whiskey. He flung the robes and furs to the ground, and men waiting beside him filled his hand with a bottle. The bottle went through the wicket, and the waiting Blackfoot had it opened and to his mouth before he had fully turned away. Several squaws were in line, jiggling with as much impatience as the men as the line moved forward. Brent remembered the Assiniboine squaws and wondered if the rest of the Blackfeet squaws were back at camp, busy hiding weapons.

At the end of an hour Hampton was soaked with sweat, and the Indians were howling with drunken laughter. He stepped aside, and another man replaced him without an interruption in the trading.

Hampton moved to where Brent stood and mopped his brow. He looked at the growing pile of robes and furs. The sacks of pemmican were heaped high to one side. "Another two hours, and we'll have everything they have. That's when they'll start offering their horses, wives, and daughters. We generally turn down the women. Some of the squaws are happy to stick a knife into a man while he's in an awkward position to defend himself."

"Do you open the gate to take their horses?"

Hampton gave him a pitying glance. "With all those drunken savages out there? No. They'll lead them here in the morning. The Indian might be filled with bitterness, but he always pays his debts."

Hampton grew more edgy as the trading neared an end. "When they haven't got anything more to trade is when you go to work."

Somebody on the walkway at the top of the wall yelled to catch Hampton's attention. The man jerked his head downward at the mass of yelling Indians below him.

Hampton walked over to the wall and handed Brent a long pole from the pile leaning against it. "Get up there with him. "You'll learn in a hurry what to do."

Other men were climbing the ladders to the walkways, and they called jokes back and forth to one another. Their faces said they enjoyed this coming time.

Brent saw Daggett and moved to join him. Daggett had the same grin of anticipation on his face. "Don't be gentle with the bastards, Brent."

Brent stared down at the crazed mass of men below him. The Indians shrieked with drunken laughter or yowled with rage as they beat on the closed wicket. Many of them showed marks of fighting, and the bright red blood stood out vividly on their bodies.

Daggett spat at them. "One of them will get the idea he can get inside by climbing the walls. Here comes the first one." He moved a few feet so as to be directly over the man.

Two of the Indian's companions lifted and threw him toward the top. The brave got a handhold between the sharpened posts and drew himself up. He tried to force his body between the pointed stakes.

Daggett let him raise his torso a little more, then jabbed viciously at the face. The end of the pole hit the Indian about the jawline and jarred him loose from the wall. He lit on his back in a bone-cracking fall and lay there dazed,

80

staring vaguely about. The Indians went into howls of laughter as the brave got to his feet and limped away.

All along the wall other traders were pushing Indians off the wall. Those who weren't. battered too much by the fall tried it again.

Daggett's eyes were fever bright. "The bastards never learn. Here comes your first one."

Brent put the end of his pole against the man's chest. He pushed instead of jabbing, and the man retained his hold.

Daggett's face twisted in disgust. "Not that way." He shoved Brent aside and slammed the end of the pole into the Indian's chest. The last glimpse Brent had of the Indian on the wall was a mouth open wide with its screaming.

He looked down, and the Indian couldn't get up. The man dragged himself along, and one leg trailed at a queer angle behind him.

"I wish I'd have broken your goddam neck," Daggett yelled after him.

It didn't take much of that to convince the Indians the walls couldn't be carried that way. They withdrew a short distance and spent several minutes in earnest talk.

Daggett dropped his pole to the ground. "They'll shoot into the fork next. It never varies." He pointed to the two men standing behind the cannon and mountain howitzer. "A little of that will change their minds fast." He swore at the sun and wiped his face. "Does this change your mind about wanting to work here?"

Brent shook his head. That was a lie. His mind was changed from the first minute he had seen Fort Whoop-up, but he couldn't do anything about it.

"I see you're still hanging around Hampton."

Brent's face flamed with sudden anger. "Damn it. He was only telling me what was going on."

Daggett gave him a hard, cold survey. "Keep it that way." Something else was on his mind, but he let it go at that.

About two dozen of the Indians advanced again, and they were armed. They had to get close to the fort to be able to reach it with those old muskets.

The men on the walkways ducked down, and bullets gouged the walls and dug holes in the compound.

Brent didn't see the cannonfire, but he heard its sullen

boom. It gouged out a great crater, and the gunner's aim was pretty good. It kicked earth all over a bunch of the Indians, and their howling was cut off short as they turned and fled. The howitzer dropped a shell right behind them.

Daggett straightened from his crouching position. He eyed the fleeing Indians. "They'll be back."

Brent didn't think so. Surely by now the Indians knew they couldn't take the fort with the kind of weapons they had.

Daggett saw the skepticism in his face. "They got one more thing to try." He bit a chunk off of a plug of tobacco. "They go through the same thing every time."

Brent stared out over the wall in disbelief. A dozen Blackfeet were creeping towards the stockade. They carried bows, and the long arrows in them flamed at the end. They had to get close to reach the fort with their arrows, and a half-dozen riflemen waited cooly, rifle butts snugged to their shoulders.

Daggett spat a stream of brown juice. "They always hope to burn down the fort. It'll cost them three or four braves before they give it up."

The creeping Indians came up to one knee, tilted the arrows toward the sky, and released them. The flaming tips made a swishing sound as they sailed over the walls. Most of the arrows landed harmlessly in the compound and guttered out there. A couple of them hit wood, and the flames licked at the sun-dried surfaces. Men dipped buckets of water out of carefully placed barrels and ran toward the tiny fires. They tossed the contents of the buckets onto the flames, and the water swept them away. The flames hadn't been given enough time to even char the wood.

Brent had been watching the arrows, and he didn't see the riflemen fire. His head whipped around at the crack of the rifles. Two Indians slumped to the ground, and the others broke in wild flight.

Daggett chuckled. "They're convinced now. They've tried everything they know."

Brent thought Daggett was wrong, for more people were rushing toward the post. Then he realized they were squaws. My God, he thought. Hampton won't let them fire on the squaws.

Daggett looked regretful. "We could punish them pretty good, but Hampton will stop it."

"Hold your fire," Hampton bellowed, and Daggett's nod said, See?

The squaws dragged off the two fallen braves, and their wailing drifted back to Brent.

"It's all over now." Daggett sounded sorry. "The sober squaws will get their men into the brush to sleep it off. They won't wake up until morning."

Brent stared unseeingly. He had just witnessed what the trade whiskey did to Indian minds. Everything they had done had been suicidal, particularly this attempt with the fire arrows. They had crept upon the post as though they had been under cover, and there hadn't been enough to hide a rabbit.

Daggett guessed what he was thinking. "It took a lot of cutting to clear the ground around the fort."

Brent didn't answer him. Whoop-up had stripped everything of value from them and added broken bones and two dead to top it off. It was a brutal lesson, and surely it wouldn't have to be repeated. Brent said what he was thinking. "They'll never come back again."

Daggett disagreed. "They'd be back in a couple of days if they had anything to trade. Once an Injun gets a taste for this whiskey, he can't stay away from it. Hell, if they learned as fast as you say, we'd be out of business long ago."

Brent climbed slowly down to the ground, feeling strangely exhausted. He suddenly knew a murderous hatred for every man in this post. They had used a people's weakness for their profit. But then, those hadn't been people to these men. They were animals, and their living and dying was no more bothersome than that of a buzzing fly.

The post got very drunk, celebrating the success of the trading day. Brent lay on his cot, listening to the revelry. Twice, he heard the rattle of pistol fire and guessed that the whiskey had recalled some minor disagreement and enflamed it. He hoped they killed each other off.

He found Hampton in the morning, and Hampton's face had a queer, drawn kind of sickness. He wondered if Hampton had drunk with the others, or if it was something else putting the sickness in him.

Hampton shook his head. "It wound up as it always does. A man killed and another wounded. If I didn't get fresh men continually, we'd be down to nothing after a few trades."

A lookout yelled, "They're bringing the horses in."

"Let's wind this up. Then I've got to send some wagons and the horses to Benton."

Brent was with him when the Indians turned their horses over, paying off their debts. He had never looked at a sorrier bunch of people. Their faces showed how sick their bellies were. They begged for a drink of whiskey and were coldly refused. But Hampton did give them a little food to get them on their way. Brent saw Daggett sneer at the softness. He watched the Blackfeet straggle away, afoot, sick, and broke.

"How will they live?"

Brent's question put a flare of irritation on Hampton's face. "On the roots that the squaws dig. Until they can make another hunt. By God, I'd like to hear him scream about yesterday's trade."

He swung away, and Brent watched him with speculative eyes. Wasn't he ever going to get that name out of the man?

12

MAJOR JAMES F. MACLEOD was a short, blocky man with a weather-roughened face. He had a vitality that wouldn't let him sit still for long. He paced the corridor before the hearing room, popping his knuckles. Upon what the committee inside that room decided depended the law and security of northwest Canada.

He passed the young man sitting in a chair and burst out, "My God, is it going to take them all day?"

Lieutenant Thad Samson grinned cynically. "You know how Parliament moves, sir. The politicians love to argue over every period. I often wonder how government ever gets anything done."

He was twenty years younger than Macleod, clear-eyed and fresh-complexioned. He had a lean, young toughness. He looked easy and composed, but in his way he was strung as tight as the Major. He wanted the Corps as badly as Macleod.

"Did you tell them about the massacre, sir?"

Macleod sat down beside him. "I used every word I could think of to make them see it as I saw it." His eyes were frozen as he recalled the scene. "Forty helpless men, women, and children slaughtered."

Samson had heard the story before, but he said, "Tell me about it, sir." Maybe the telling would keep the Major from pacing.

Macleod's face was passionately angry. "Those vermin." His fist was a hard rock. "If only I had the power to stamp out every whiskey trader on earth. Sixteen white men from Fort Benton set up their trading camp on the eastern edge of Montagne de Cypres, the Cypress Hills, fifty miles north of the Montana border. Fifty lodges of the Assiniboines set up to trade with them. After they had traded everything they had and while they were helpless with drink, the whites, probably drunk themselves, accused them of stealing some of their horses. The Montanans opened fire from hidden positions in the brush. I know they killed forty of them. I saw the bodies. I don't know how many they wounded. The survivors fled into the hills. I found a few of them, but they ran at the sight of me. I was a white man."

"Were the traders caught?"

"A few of them. But the evidence against them was held to be insufficient, and they escaped conviction. If that committee can't see the need of a police force to control the country, that massacre will happen again and again."

"They'll see it, sir."

Macleod gave him a sour look. "I wish I could be as certain."

Another hour dragged by, and Macleod was wearing a groove in the floor with his pacing.

Then the hearing-room door opened, and Colonel Patrick Robertson Ross, the Adjutant General of the Dominion, came out into the hall. He was a tall man with erect bearing and hair that was almost white. His face was inordinately grave.

Macleod jumped to his feet, his face flaming. "They couldn't see the need, sir? We were turned down."

Ross laughed. "My little joke, Major. I wanted to sweat you another minute. You painted a graphic picture in there. We were discussing details. That's why it took so long."

The graveness came back at the elation flooding Macleod's face. "You've asked for a big job, Major."

"Give me the men and the authority, sir, and I can handle it."

Ross nodded. "We think you can. Sit down, man, sit down. You have been appointed assistant commissioner with full powers to handle any situation as you see fit. Let me warn you. These offenders are mostly Americans. If they're turned over to their courts, they'll be turned free before you get back across the border."

Macleod's face was grim. "I know, sir."

"Good! Then we're in complete understanding. I am to draw up plans for a mounted regiment of five hundred and fifty men. They are to wear scarlet coats, because the Indians remember too well the green-coated Winnipeg garrison. We want those scarlet coats to be a symbol of friendship, not punishment. We thought of calling the regiment the Canadian Mounted Rifles, but that has a military connotation, and it could alarm the United States. To emphasize its civilian character, we decided to call it the North West Mounted Police. The crest of the corps will be a buffalo head and its motto, 'Maintiens le droit.' You are to take a hundred and fifty men into the country between the Cypress Hills and the Rockies."

Samson whooped with joy, then looked crestfallen. Ross frowned sternly at him, then laughed. "I know how you feel. If my age didn't demand dignity, I would have whooped myself when the committee made its decision."

He faced Macleod. "How soon can you start?"

Macleod's eyes shone with a hard joy. "Just as soon as I can select my men and gather the necessary supplies."

"Spare nothing, Major. You've been given full power to draw on the government for anything you need."

Macleod looked back at the long column of men and supply wagons behind him. They were the Dominion's finest, hand selected by him. Every horse was the best obtainable, every one of them more than fifteen hands high. Each man carried a pistol and cartridges in his belt and a Snider carbine in a boot on his saddle. What was far better, they knew how to use them. The saddles were the U. S. McClellan with the high cantle and slotted tree. The uniform consisted of a red tunic, black breeches, and a pillbox cap. A white helmet for dress was packed in the rolls behind the saddles. Black boots and an overcoat with cape completed the outfit.

Macleod's heart swelled with pride. It had been a difficult and dangerous trip, much of it traveled through outlaw country. The hostile Blackfeet were always a threat. They hadn't been attacked; the size of the force was a deterrent, but it could happen at any moment. He had a right to his pride. Not a man had faltered, accepting willingly any hardship that came along. Men and horses had gotten through in surprisingly good shape. That was because the men had been trained to take care of themselves and their animals.

Samson rode beside him. "Looking at them makes you feel sort of good, doesn't it, sir?"

"It does," Macleod said crisply. "I wish we could hunt action right away." At Samson's evident disappointment, he added, "We've got to think of shelter for men and animals first."

"You mean build a post?" Samson's tone showed he was thinking of the time it would take.

"That, or buy one. Fort Whoop-up is twenty miles ahead. I'd like to look it over."

"Is that the big post?"

Macleod nodded. "The biggest of them all. Buying it would be one way of putting it out of business."

Macleod saw that Samson wasn't sure whether or not he was joking. "I'm not joking. I'm authorized to offer up to ten thousand dollars for it."

Samson's eyes widened. That was a fabulous sum. "Will they sell it?"

"No." The word was decisive. "They'll make twice that much out of it in a year. Would you sell?"

"Maybe they won't be in business in another year."

"I'm planning on it, Thad."

Macleod left the troops two miles from Whoop-up and ordered them to go into camp for the night. He selected

Samson to ride with him. "When we come back, I'll know what we have to do. I don't think the traders know we're in the country yet. I want to look at their faces when they see us and find out why we're here."

Samson grinned. "You don't think they'll welcome us?"

"Oh, they'll welcome us all right. Our concern is turning it off before it gets too hot."

Both men looked Fort Whoop-up over thoroughly as they rode to the wicket in the gate. "They built well," Macleod said thoughtfully.

He reined up before the closed wicket, and when it opened, said, "I want to see your commanding officer."

"Are you outta your head?" a voice jeered. "This ain't no army post."

"All right, then. Your manager, or whatever you call the man in charge."

"Who are you?"

"Major Macleod. Of the North West Mounted Police."

Samson's eyes gleamed at the long following silence. It might be because Macleod's announcement stunned the man behind the wicket.

The voice came again. "He's got no business with you."

"I think he has," Macleod snapped. "You tell him I'm here."

The wicket closed, and it seemed they waited an interminable time before the gate opened.

"He'll see you," the bearded man said. He pointed to the fat man standing before the log building against the inside wall.

"What's his name?"

The man's face turned sullen at the note of authority in Macleod's voice. "Hampton," he muttered.

The traders made a lane reaching halfway to where Hampton stood. Macleod and Samson rode down it at a slow, measured pace, ignoring the remarks thrown at them.

"Ain't they fancy?" one of the men said.

"Dressed up real pretty," another agreed.

"They can't be real. Hey, what are you two playing at?"

Samson's face mirrored his disgust at the slovenly condition of the post. "They live like animals."

Macleod classified it further. "No, pigs." His eyes swept the compound, taking in every detail.

How would you like to have them under your command, sir?"

Macleod's lips pressed tightly together. "Not a one of them could clean up behind our horses. Look them over good, Thad. These are the kind of men we'll be dealing with."

Samson looked up and down the lane. "I'd say it will be hard to get anything through their heads."

"The business end of a rifle will do that."

They rode straight up to Hampton and stopped. Neither man made a move to dismount.

Brent and Daggett stood a few feet from Hampton. Brent prodded Daggett. "Who are they?" he whispered.

"I'll be damned if I know. But they sure rode in here like they owned the place."

Macleod's eyes drilled into Hampton. "Mr. Hampton? Are you in charge here?"

Hampton nodded warily to both questions.

"I'm Major Macleod. Of the North West Mounted Police. I'm empowered to buy this post from you."

Hampton gaped at him before he recovered himself. "How much will you pay?"

"Ten thousand dollars. Cash!"

Hampton broke into raucous laughter. "You couldn't touch it for three times that."

"I thought your answer would be something like that." Macleod leaned forward and stabbed a finger at Hampton. "My advice to you would be to take it. Because a year from now, you will not be operating it."

Hampton's face twisted derisively. "Are you going to put us out of business?"

"I and my men. We are already here in force. We don't need this fort. We'll build our own." For the first time his face showed anger. "You're on Canadian soil, Mr. Hampton. Unauthorized. You have cheated and debauched the Indians too long."

"A damned Indian lover," somebody yelled from behind Macleod. He didn't even turn his head.

"Keep on the way you're going, Hampton. You'll find your crimes will earn the punishment they deserve."

He locked eyes with Hampton, and Hampton broke first. His face reddened under the knowledge that everybody here had seen it, and he tried to recover lost ground. "Why, you poor damned fool. We'll be here long after you're forgotten."

Macleod might have been looking at some strange, loathsome species. "I have a feeling you're a bad prophet, Mr. Hampton."

He wheeled his horse, and Samson caught up with him. His eyes were shining. "Beautiful, sir. You shook him up."

Macleod allowed a frosty grin to touch his face. "I doubt if mere words will do that job, Thad."

"But you had something more in mind?"

Macleod's grin broadened. "A little."

They rode back down the lane, and the remarks were louder and more abusive. They received the same attention they had the first trip through it.

Macleod turned his head as the gate slammed shut behind them. "Now I'll prophesy something. I don't think that gate will be willingly opened to us again."

Samson broke into laughter. "And that's the way you want it. May I suggest a name for the new fort? Fort Macleod."

Macleod looked pleased in spite of himself. "I don't know—"

Samson interrupted him. "You won't have much to say about it, Major. The men will outvote it" He kept stealing little glances at Macleod. This day had pleased Macleod in every way.

13

THAT NIGHT Daggett came into Brent's room. He sat down on the chair and put his boots up on Brent's bed. If he noticed Brent's frown, it didn't bother him.

"What did you think of the fancy policemen?"

Brent had been thinking about Macleod all afternoon. He had no idea what the man was going to do, but he knew Macleod meant business. "What did you think?" He wanted Daggett's opinion before he spoke.

"Did you ever look at a colder pair of eyes? I'm telling you, that was one of the toughest sonuvabitches I've ever seen."

Daggett meant it. His impression of Macleod was in his tone and solemn face. "Did you see him break Hampton? Hampton folded with everybody watching him."

Brent could nod agreement to that. Hampton had caved in under those eyes. He had tried to recover, but not a man watching was unaware of what had happened.

Daggett talked more to himself than to Brent. "I think that red-coated policeman might be just tough enough to do what he said he would." He shook his head in disbelief. "Who would have ever thought the Canadian government would send policemen out this far?"

"Will Hampton fight him?"

Daggett recrossed his feet. "Hell, no. He hasn't got the guts." He stared piercingly at Brent. "Do you still think he's the man to follow?"

That question must have been sticking in Daggett's craw, and Brent felt the familiar thrust of anger at its repetition. "Dammit, I've never said that. How many times do I have to tell you?"

Daggett held up a hand. "Okay, okay. Jesus, did you hear how much that policeman offered for this post?"

"You didn't expect Hampton to take it, did you?"

"Not if it can continue as a whiskey-trading post. But suppose the major is right in saying what he's going to do? How much will it be worth then?"

Brent shrugged. He didn't know, nor care.

Daggett answered for him. "Not a plugged dime. The whiskey draws the Indians in to trade. They wouldn't come near here without it." His eyes held a feral light. "Ten thousand dollars. Do you know how much money that is?"

Brent smiled wryly. "I can't figure that high."

"It would set a couple of smart men up for a long time. Maybe for life."

Brent's eyes sharpened. "What have you got in mind?"

Daggett stood and stretched. "Nothing, except that I don't think it would make any difference to Macleod who he bought it from. I just keep playing around with that idea."

He walked to the door and turned. "I'm not forgetting

how much I owe you. That's why I figure you've got a cut in any idea I get."

Brent stared at the closed door. Something was hatching in Daggett's mind, and he could almost draw a picture of it. If Daggett had command of the post, why couldn't he turn it over to Macleod, pocket the purchase price, and vanish? Hampton was walking on thin ice. Brent had no doubt that already Daggett was readying some plan for him, a plan that wouldn't do Hampton's health a bit of good. It might be wise for him to gradually disassociate himself from Hampton. If it came to a showdown between the two men, he would have to pick Daggett.

He resumed his staring at the ceiling. Macleod's coming into this was a new factor, and he didn't know what to do about it. He wished Moore were here to talk this over with him. Moore would know whether it was good or bad. He turned over and blew out the lantern. He hoped he could get a decent stretch of sleep that night.

Life at Whoop-up fell into a monotonous routine. Supply wagons loaded with cargoes of raw alcohol arrived at the post and left reloaded with trade goods. Whoever the boss man was, he shouldn't have cause to complain. Brent made guarded attempts to pry a name out of some of the men and met with a dismal degree of success. If they didn't know, they displayed no curiosity. Brent concluded that only Hampton and Daggett knew the name of the man who was behind Whoop-up.

He went through four more trading days, and except for the different tribes involved, they were exactly the same as the first he had seen. The Bloods came in, both north and south branches, followed by the Piegans and the Assiniboines. Brent had had a sympathy for the Blackfeet on that first day of trading. But now it was replaced by a great and growing rage. They were nothing but stupid animals. Didn't they have a spark of intelligence? Couldn't they see what was being done to them? Yet back they came, time and time again. Once they tasted whiskey, apparently their appetite for it couldn't be appeased. He spent long hours thinking about it, and the only definite conclusion he reached was that he despised the Indian blood in his veins. He found he could stand on that walkway and jab an Indian off of the wall as viciously as any man at Whoop-up. He knew he had a broken leg to his dubious credit, and he suspected a broken back by the way other Indians carried off the man. He stomped ruthlessly on any regret that tried to arise within him. The Indian deserved no better. The rationalization didn't brighten his spirits. He was striking out at his Indian blood, and that was foolish, because nothing could be done about it. The churning agony within him left his thoughts confused and hate-filled.

He came out of a building to find Hampton and Daggett less than a dozen yards from him. Their faces were close together and showed heated anger. He wondered if Daggett was pushing a quarrel and stepped back inside, not wanting to be pulled into it. Their voices were raised in anger, and only snatches of sentences came clearly to him. He heard Hampton shout something about a neighbor and lost the rest of the sentence. Were Hampton and Daggett quarreling over the presence of Macleod and his men? Macleod had picked a site twenty-eight miles from Whoop-up, and Brent had ridden out with Daggett a couple of days ago to look at it. Macleod was building with unbelievable speed. Brent was startled at the size of the force Macleod had. The men worked with disciplined efficiency, and Brent contrasted those men with the men at Whoop-up. The comparison put a wince in him.

Macleod knew they were on this hill, for Brent had seen the reflection of sunlight from glasses, but Macleod made no attempt to approach or send anybody after them.

Daggett had watched in long, thoughtful silence. "They get things done," he had finally said.

They did. Already shelter had been built for horses and a lot of the men. Quite a few tents were still up, but at the speed with which Macleod was going, those tents wouldn't be up much longer.

Daggett had turned his horse, but before he put it into faster movement he had said, "Those Mounties could be bad trouble."

It was the first time Brent had heard the term used. It wasn't a disparaging one. Daggett had all the respect in the world in his tone.

They had ridden back and reported what they had seen to Hampton. Brent remembered the pinched look that had seized Hampton's face. "What the hell do you expect me to do about it?" he had shouted.

Brent listened to the heated voices continue for a brief time longer. Yes, he thought. They're arguing about the Mounties. The term had lodged in his mind because it fitted so well. Some of the other men scoffed at Macleod's policemen, saying what a target those red coats would make. Just let them try to ride against Whoop-up. Brent recalled that cold look in Macleod's eyes. He doubted Macleod would ever be foolish enough to ride against stockade walls because of the loss it would cost him. But if he ever made such a decision, he would take the fort. He swore a raging oath against Lucas Moore's name for putting him here. He had no desire to shoot at Macleod's men, but his position might force him to.

He no longer heard the voices arguing, and he stepped outside again. Hampton was crossing the compound, and his anger showed in the way his weight came down heavily with each stride. Daggett leaned against a wall, and he jerked his head at Brent.

Brent reluctantly approached him. He was in no mood to talk to the man.

For a man who had just been in a heated argument, Daggett seemed in a high good mood. "Hog's doing a lot of worrying these days. He should have taken the Mounties' offer and sold out."

So that was still in his mind. "Would you have?" Brent really had no interest in the answer.

"I'd have jumped at it. Let's go get a drink."

The only thing available was the trade whiskey, and Brent shook his head.

Daggett's face had a mocking cast. "Are you afraid of the stuff?"

Brent's face hardened. "Should I be?"

Daggett beat a hasty retreat. "Everybody's so damned touchy these days. I was just wondering—"

"Don't," Brent said bluntly.

Daggett was right about everybody being touchy. Crosscurrents rippled through the post, and the men were ready to jump at one another's throats. Last week another man had been killed. Hampton had raved about it, and he had tried to

94

pour work on them as a solution. He had tried to keep the men busy from morning to night, and they were rebellious under his orders. That wouldn't solve what was bothering these men. The loneliness, the cooped up living, and the constant danger was a huge grindstone fraying their nerves. If things continued this way for too long, Macleod wouldn't have to do anything about Whoop-up. One of these days it would blow up with one big bang. And who would be sorry about that? Brent growled to himself.

"What the hell's gotten into you? A man can't even talk to you anymore."

"Then don't try."

Brent watched the murderous rage fill Daggett's eyes and didn't give a damn. Maybe he was pushing Daggett too hard. He didn't care about that, either.

Daggett broke off a gusty puff of breath and spun on his heel. He stomped away from Brent.

Brent watched him until he was out of sight. One way or another, continuing this mood between him and Daggett could bring a release from Whoop-up. If he killed Daggett, there no longer would be a reason for him to stay. And if Daggett killed him, that wiped it out too. He thought the madness must be touching him, also, even to be considering it. He had a simple way out. All he had to do was to ride away from here. He thought of Moore and of what the man had done for him. He cursed Lucas Moore with all of the fervor in his system. Why should that hold him? But he knew he wasn't going to ride away, not until he had finished a job.

He passed the blacksmith shop and stopped as he heard the pounding that came from it. Upon impulse he stepped inside. Haines was one of the most amiable men on the post.

His back was toward Brent as he stood at the forge. He was stripped to the waist, for the enclosure was stiflingly hot. He was a brawny man, and Brent watched the play of massive muscles. Haines pounded at the piece of metal, and Brent wondered at the savagery in the blows. Haines wasn't in an amiable mood today.

He turned to reheat the metal in the forge and saw Brent. "What the hell do you want?"

He was a broad-faced man with a flattened nose bent to one side of his face. If that came from a fight, Brent wondered what man had ever been foolish enough to get into an argument with Haines.

Brent shrugged. "Nothing. I just had a few empty minutes."

Haines worked the bellows, and the flames danced higher. "By God, I wish I had. That goddamned Hampton keeps piling work on me." He had left the tongs in the fire, and they were glowing as he picked up the piece of metal with them. Holding the tongs in his gloved hand, he placed the piece of metal on the anvil "Don't stand around cluttering up my shop."

Brent looked away from those fierce eyes. It wouldn't take much for Haines to throw him out. He shook his head as he walked outside. When Haines was this quarrelsome, the madness in the fort was rampant.

This damned place, Brent thought as he moved along If any man in it had a lick of brains, he would run like hell from it. Brent guessed he belonged with the rest of them His head was empty, too.

14

The two men led horses that carried grisly burdens The dangling bodies swung with each step the animals took They looked like bundles of rags, rags that had ominous stains all over them. The bundles threatened to slip off at any second.

The taller of the two men spat a stream of tobacco juice. He couldn't have said how far back it had been since he had had a haircut, and his shaggy beard hid the lower half of his face. His hat was a decrepit, battered thing, and a lock of hair stuck out through a hole in the crown. His clothing had gone far beyond serviceable wear, and patch upon patch wasn't doing too good a job of holding it together. The clothing, like his face, was indescribably filthy. It was covered with grease stains, and wolf blood had dried to crusty black smears. Compared to the rest of his outfit, his boots were surprisingly good.

His companion was a smaller replica of him with perhaps his clothing even more ragged. And his hair had a reddish shade. Both of them trudged along heavily, showing several miles behind them.

"You got any chewing tobacco, Jed?" the smaller man asked.

"Goddamn it, Parney. I'm sick of supplying you tobacco. Don't you ever buy anything?"

Parney Means grinned, showing bad teeth. Jed Riker didn't mean anything by that. He always grumbled, but he always came across.

Parney walked along patiently, letting his request dig deeper into Jed's head. Pretty soon Jed wouldn't be able to stand it any longer, and he would dig out part of a plug.

"You worthless sonuvabitch. I don't know why I don't shoot you." But Jed's hand was digging into his pocket.

Parney hid the laughter in his eyes. He had learned from long experience that if Jed saw it, he could turn as stubborn as a mule.

He didn't reach for the plug until it was well in view. He mustn't show too much haste. Jed dropped it into the outstretched hand with a grumbled, "Worthless."

Parney judiciously eyed the plug. Jed was going to have to get himself a new one pretty soon. He didn't bother to brush off the lint and dirt sticking to the tobacco. And he didn't bother to find an unchawed-on place.

Jed snatched the remains from him. "Are you trying to make your supper on it?"

Parney didn't try to reply. His mouth was too full. He moved the chaw around in his mouth, getting it between his good teeth so he could masticate it. He took a lot of abuse from Jed for a puny chew of tobacco, but he considered his gain greater than his loss.

Jed's face resumed its gloomy cast. "I sure hate to bring them into camp."

Parney understood the uneasiness in Jed's eyes. He felt the same way. "Cass put a store in Billy. He's purely going to raise hell. Jed, do you suppose he might blame us?" He argued against his own question. "Why dammit it, all we did was bring them in."

Jed shook his head. "Who knows what that crazy Cass will do?"

Neither man showed any sorrow for the dead men. They had seen too much quick, violent death on these savage prairies.

"I even thought of leaving them out there, Parney."

Parney gave that grave consideration. "It might have been smarter. But it's too late to do anything about it now. They see us coming in."

"I see them," Jed snarled.

A group of men stood at the camp's edge, shading their eyes against the sun. The camp was set on the Spitzee, and Jed and Parney were close enough to hear the splashing of the river against the rocks.

Parney couldn't let the subject of Cass' reaction to Billy's death alone. Neither of them had mentioned old man Greer. Neither of them thought much about him, one way or the other. Both Billy and Greer had been killed by rifle shots, and the bodies had been mutilated and scalped. The unshod prints showed that the Indians had gotten out of there in a hurry, maybe becaused they feared other wolfers were around.

He heaved a sigh, and it was out of deference to the bad moment that was ahead. "Jed, I still say it's better to have a clean hole through you than being stuck full of arrows like some I've seen."

Jed put fierce eyes on him. "You tell that to Cass. He'll get a lot of good out of it." He, too, sighed. Billy had been only eighteen years old. As Parney said, Cass Culver put a store in his brother.

They splashed across the river, and now everybody in camp was crowding forward. Without Billy and Greer there were twenty-three men left. The camp was a sad, sorry one, its comforts few and primitive. But then, what wolfer was ever concerned about comfort? He would have stared in amazement if anybody had mentioned the word to him. His life was a series of days filled with danger and hardships, and he didn't expect to find comforts on the plains. Those would come when enough wolf pelts were accumulated to take to

Benton. There he could find his comforts in the drunken revels that soon stripped him of his hard-earned money. But they left him with a lot of memories to tell and retell around a night's campfire. His mouth would twist hungrily as he recalled and told how this woman or that one looked and acted, and the words, "By God, did I make her howl!" were used again and again. Afterwards, it was the plains again. But he had something that shortened the long hours there; he had his memory of the last trip into town and another trip to look forward to.

Cass Culver approached clear to the water's edge. The others jammed up behind him, but none dared crowd or jostle him. He was a giant of a man with a terrible, unpredictable temper. The wolfers said admiringly that Cass Culver could squeeze the life out of a grizzly bear. Many of them had felt the weight of his hand. The few who were unwise enough to object were dead.

He stood there bareheaded, the scar that started above an eyebrow and disappeared into the matted beard, showing purplish as the sun caught it at the right angle. He stood there without moving, and a man couldn't see the lifting and falling of his chest. Only his eyes seemed alive, and they were reddish malignant things. Men glanced uneasily at each other. They remembered when Cass had brought Billy onto the plains three years ago. The kid was the only family Cass had, and he had overindulged him. Nobody was going to grieve too much about Billy. He had been an arrogant, smart-alecky kid, doing anything that came into his head, knowing Cass was there to back him up. He had ridden out this morning against Cass' orders, and he had gotten himself killed. That was a morsel to chew with satisfaction.

"Billy?" The name forced itself out without consciousness. Cass knew it was Billy.

"Yes, it is, Cass. We brought him in because we knowd you'd want it that way."

Jed groaned silently. He wished he had thought to tell Parney to keep his mouth shut, for once he opened his mouth it was like blowing a great hole in a dam.

Cass turned that fierce red glare on him.

"We knowd you'd want to see him once more, Cass. We knowd—"

Cass slashed a heavy hand into Parney's face, driving him back a step. He must have been gathering volume for his roar for some time. "Get away from me."

Parney held a hand to his broken lips but showed no resentment. The blood flowed through his beard, gathering at the point of it, and dripped onto his shirt. "I don't blame you, Cass. I know just how you feel about Billy."

Those eyes turned insane, and Parney was wise enough to read them correctly. He had a step on Cass, and he used it well. He scuttled up the bank, and Cass' blow missed him by a hairsbreadth.

Cass didn't follow him. He stood staring at the burdened horse with unseeing eyes.

Jed plodded up the bank, leading the horse with Greer. Cass never even glanced at him or the horse. As Jed caught up with Parney, he said, "You crazy goddamned fool. Were you trying to get us both killed?"

Parney put an aggrieved look on him. "Hell, I was just trying to help him a little. I know if it was me, I'd want somebody—"

"Will you shut up?"

Jed led the horse to a grove of poplar trees and laid old man Greer in the shade. He covered him with a dirty, ragged piece of canvas, for the flies were bad. It wouldn't be thirty seconds until they found him, and a man wouldn't be able to see Greer for the flies.

He came back and joined the others. They squatted on their heels, talking in uneasy murmers. A man couldn't go a minute without his eyes straying across the camp to where Cass sat beside Billy's body.

"Damn, I hope he doesn't get drunk," one man said. Cass Culver had gone on some memorable drunks, and men and material always suffered. And those drunks had had nothing like this behind them.

"He won't," somebody answered him. "We drank up all the whiskey last night."

A sigh of relief ran among them. "Who do you figure did it?" Duke Eckart asked.

"Indians." Parney never missed a chance to grab the conversation.

Eckart gave him a pitying look. "You ain't got enough

100

brains to blow a fart out. We know that. What kind of Indians?"

Jed gave Parney a warning look to keep quiet. "We don't know. The only sign we found was unshod hoof tracks. We didn't try to trail them. They took Billy's and Greer's horses."

Eckart shook his head gloomily. "It's getting so it isn't safe to be out on these prairies."

Heads nodded solemnly. That was a fact, for sure.

Cass remained in that motionless position for better than an hour, then he got to his feet and approached them. Every face had that same apprehensive look.

Cass ignored Parney and looked at Jed. "Was there any trail?"

Jed shook his head. The fewer words he could use in answering Cass, the better off he was.

"Did you look for their horses?"

Jed spread out his hands. "They were gone, Cass."

A wild burst of rage twisted Cass' face. "Billy was killed by a modern rifle."

Jed nodded. The old trade muskets would have torn a bigger hole.

"I'll kill every goddamned Indian I can find," Cass shouted.

Again they looked at each other uneasily. If Cass started out on some crazy war of his own, they would have to ride with him. Not a man of them would dare to refuse.

"The Indians did it, Cass." An idea was forming in Jed's head, and he struggled to smooth it out. "They did it all right, but they're not the ones responsible."

Those eyes slammed against him, and for a moment Jed was afraid the insane rage behind them was going to wash over him. "Who's responsible?"

"The damned whiskey traders. They'll trade modern rifles and bullets, won't they? They killed Billy."

Cass' chest heaved. "By God, you're right. Those stinking Indians couldn't have gotten close to Billy with muskets. I'll kill every rotten trader in the country."

Jed's face showed his dismay. In trying to take Cass' mind off of Indians, he had only made matters worse. Cass was crazy enough to lead a charge against the walls of Whoop-up. And Jed know there were cannon and scores of modern rifles behind them. They would be cut down before they got halfway across that clearing.

He couldn't keep the squeak out of his voice. "Cass, we can't go up against them walls."

Cass looked at him coldly. "Did I say anything like that?"

Jed feebly shook his head.

Cass sneered at him. "You wouldn't be afraid to go along if I showed you how to get inside?"

Again Jed shook his head.

"They can't stay behind those walls all the time, can they? They got to send out hunting parties, or supply wagons have to come in. We'll lie in wait and capture a hunting party or a wagon. I think I can convince whatever we take to get those gates open for us."

He spat at the ground, and it was an offensive gesture intended for all of them. "You'd take everything we could find in that post, wouldn't you?"

Eyes gleamed at the thought of material things Fort Whoop-up held.

"I thought you would. Now get a shovel and help me bury Billy."

He strode away without looking at the poplar grove.

15

HAMPTON WAS a lonely man. And each hour he stayed in this room the closer the walls moved to him. He made another turn around it, pounding a fist into a palm. He knew the men talked contemptuously about him, but he didn't care, for he despised them. Scum, he thought. Nothing but scum. He purposely kept the breach between them and him as wide as possible, even eating most of his meals in solitude. He slapped angrily at his belly. He was going to have to order new pants. He could hardly get the waistband of this pair buttoned. He knew what he was doing to himself. To compensate for the lack of other satisfactions, he ate too much. He had gained a lot of weight in the last few months.

Daggett never failed to call him Hog, and the men snickered. He wished he had the nerve to call Daggett out and kill him. But he was afraid of the man. Daggett had something in mind. It glinted in his eyes each time Daggett looked at him. He cursed Nader in a vicious burst of rage. He was still convinced Nader had a definite purpose in sending Daggett here, though passing time was weakening that conviction. Surely, if the man had a definite order, he would have acted before now. A hopeful idea was growing in his head. Perhaps Daggett hadn't been sent here to take over, maybe he had been sent here because he was in disgrace with Nader.

He wished he had somebody to talk to about it. He had been drawn to Brent Bargen when he first arrived, but that was weakening fast. The man was uncommunicative, almost sullen. To hell with him, Hampton thought. He would treat him as he did all the others. He would work his ass off. Bargen had had his chance. If he kicked it away, that was his loss.

A wave of self-pity and loneliness engulfed him. What made him stay in this filthy business? He had gone into it because, at the time, there was nothing else. He had promised himself that he would quit at the end of last year, and he knew why he hadn't. Money! He was amassing a tidy sum; when he left this country, he could reestablish himself, and this time he wouldn't make the same foolish mistake that had wrecked him before.

His face brightened. He would quit with the arrival of cold weather, and that wasn't too far away. He would ride out of this post and leave the scum to rot here. And he wouldn't weaken, no matter how much more money Nader promised him.

Even with his solution to his problem in hand, the room was still oppressive. He had to get out of it, and better still, off of the post.

He picked a rifle from its rack of horns and walked out into the compound. He would give Bargen one more chance. He found him in the stable area, pitchforking manure. Bargen would jump at anything to get out of that.

He gestured, beckoning him away from the others. Bargen had that sullen impassiveness in his face again, and Hampton pushed his rising anger back.

"How'd you like to ride out with me and see if we can't

pick up a deer? Wouldn't some fresh meat taste good?"
Certainly, there was some danger in it, but he wouldn't stray
too far from the fort. A man could find as much or more
danger inside these walls.

He couldn't believe it. Bargen's head was shaking from
side to side. Bargen was turning him down.

His face flamed, and his breathing turned ragged. "I could
order you to go."

"Yes." The word was flat and uncompromising.

The other men watched curiously, and it enraged Hampton
further.

"Why you stupid—" He broke it off before he completely
lost control.

He saddled his horse and rode out of the stables. He
thought he heard laughter behind him, and he quivered with
rage. That settled it. Bargen belonged in the same class as
the others.

He turned in the saddle and looked back at the fort after
several hundred yards. He wished he could blow the damned
thing up. His eyes picked up a wicked gleam. Maybe that was
what he would do. Maybe he would blow the damned place
up the day he quit.

He sucked on the idea as he rode, getting tremendous
subsistence from it. There was enough powder in the powder
room to do the job. In his mind he could hear the great roar
of the explosion and see the fierce, fiery blossoming before
the walls shattered into matchsticks. He was almost happy
again.

He had ridden into brush and timber and paid but absent
attention to his surroundings. He didn't really want to find a
deer; he didn't want to be bothered with the trouble of
bleeding it, then hoisting it on horseback. But he had needed
this trip; he needed it to clear his mind and to set himself a
new, hard purpose.

They were all around him, and it happened too suddenly to
get a fixed hold on any thought. They sprang up out of the
brush, and he had never seen such evil faces. His tongue
froze, and his heart pounded like a runaway hammer in a
throat that had suddenly gone too dry.

If he had thought of trying to spur away from them, it was
too late now, for one of them had hold of the bridle. And if

104

that wasn't enough to halt him, the menacing rifles were. My God! There must have been better than twenty of them. The thought of resistance died as quickly as it entered his mind. Even if his pistol had already been in his hand, he would have been cut down before he could get more than two or three of them.

"What do you want?" He cursed his mouse squeak of a voice.

A giant of a man pushed through the others and stood beside him. He had a wild triumph on his face, and he looked around at the others before he asked, "What did I tell you? Didn't it work?" His eyes came back to Hampton and bored through him.

"Who are you?"

"Hoge Hampton." He couldn't raise his voice from that squeak.

"By God," the giant roared, "we've got the big one. Do you know me?"

Hampton shook a dazed head. All feeling was fleeing from him, leaving him numb. He only knew he was in deadly danger.

A huge hand clamped on his arm and jerked. It pulled him from his saddle, then let him fall to the ground. The impact slammed the air from his lungs, and his eyes swam.

"I'm Cass Culver. You'll know me now."

Hampton's soul shrieked in terror. He had heard of the man. Culver led the wildest pack of wolvers these plains had ever known, and men shook their heads when they talked about him.

That savage face looked down at him. "Won't you?"

Before Hampton could even try to reply, a boot toe thudded into his ribs. Its force left him sick, and he thought he was going to vomit. He choked back the rising waves of nausea and almost whimpered. Oh God, that kick must have broken some ribs.

"You son-of-a-bitch. You will trade rifles to the Indians. You killed my brother. I'll kick you to pieces."

Hampton didn't know what he was talking about, but the paroxysm of rage twisting Culver's face said he meant every word of it. The foot drew back for another kick, and Hampton closed his eyes. It had been a long time since he had prayed, and he couldn't think of a prayer now. All he could say over and over was, Oh, God. Oh, God.

A bearded man seized Culver's arm, stopping the kick. He hung on resolutely, despite the quick transfer of rage to him.

"Cass, if you mark him up too much, won't it hurt our chances of getting inside the fort?"

Hampton opened his eyes at the sound of the voice. He saw the fury weaken on Culver's face. "Damned if you're not right, Jed. I'll save that pleasure for later."

His face was almost normal. "I'll tell you what you're going to do, Hampton. You're going to climb back on your horse and take four of us back to your fort. You're going to tell them we're new men you've hired and to open up. There's going to be a rifle pointed at your backbone every second, and if you make the smallest mistake, that rifle's going to blow your backbone into shreds. Do you understand?"

Hamptotn nodded numbly. It gave him a little more life, it was a reprieve from vicious punishment. After one look at these wolfers, his men could see that he would never hire likes of them. Riflemen would pick them off, and he would enjoy seeing every one of them die.

Hope flooded him, and he scrambled to his feet, trying to ignore the stabbing grab of pain in his side.

The one called Jed grinned. "I believe he understands you, Cass."

"He'd better keep it that way." Cass selected three men and turned to the others. "Creep up as close as you can without being seen. Come arunning when you hear a rifle shot. We're going to capture us a fort."

No, you won't, you bastard, Hampton thought. You won't get inside the gate.

There was a small discussion about his keeping his rifle and pistol, and Culver ended it. "Let him keep them. It'll look more natural that way."

And I'll empty them into you, Hampton vowed.

He rode in front of the four, and at Culver's order he made it an easy, natural gait. They rode close behind him, and he knew where a rifle was aimed.

He was sweating profusely as he approached the gate, yet his skin felt cold and clammy. Who was on it at the moment?

106

Whoever it was, he hoped the man was paying keen attention. Surely by now he had seen what the men behind him were and had alerted the others.

Culver's low voice carried to him. "Make it good, mister."

Hampton gulped. If his voice betrayed him now, he was lost. He made it as much a roar as he could. "What the hell's the matter with you? Open that gate."

"Who's that with you?"

Hampton's heart plummeted. Trimble was on the gate, and he was a slow-witted man. He had probably watched their approach without saying a word to anybody else.

"Four men I hired." Hampton's flesh around his backbone was dying in anticipation of a bullet crashing into it. Soon that dying would spread all over him.

He made a tremendous effort and steadied his voice. "Trimble, if you don't open that gate, I'll break your neck."

He learned that a man could live a lifetime in a second. The gate swung slowly open. He cast a despairing glance at Culver. Culver's face was split in a broad grin.

Brent was crossing the compound when the gate swung open. He glanced toward it with only ordinary curiosity. Who were the four men Hampton was bringing in with him? They were a damned tough-looking bunch.

The four split, covering all the men in sight, and Brent's jaw sagged as he looked at the leveled rifles.

"Call the rest of them out here," the big dirty man beside Hampton said. He reached over and took Hampton's pistol and rifle. "Be damned careful how you do it."

Hampton raised his voice, and men came out of the buildings onto the compound. They stared at the menacing rifles with wide, wondering eyes.

"Is that all of them?" the big man demanded.

Hampton shut his eyes in frantic concentration. Every time he counted them, he got a different answer. He went over the faces, trying to see if a familiar one was missing. He just couldn't tell for sure.

Culver jabbed the rifle muzzle into his painful side, and it pulled a bleat out of him "You want to die right here?"

"Yes." Hampton strengthened the word. "Yes, they're all here."

"Line them up against that wall over there. Tell every man to throw his guns on the ground in front of him. If one even hesitates, he's dead."

Hampton gave the order, and pistols plopped into the dust. He didn't have to urge haste, for every man was certain a rifle muzzle was pointed directly at him.

Hampton shivered. He was naked in a cold, biting wind.

"Jed," Culver said, "go out the gate and let off a round. No, make it two so they'll be sure and hear it."

Brent stood beside Daggett, and Daggett's face was twisted with malevolence. "The dirty bastard sold us out," he hissed.

Brent had no doubt Hampton had been forced to sell them out, but Daggett wouldn't consider that. He looked at Hampton's face, and it had the color of rain-soaked dough. Some kind of mortal fear had clamped on Hampton, and maybe they all should be feeling it. He knew he felt alone and helpless. Hampton had stressed how dangerous the wolfers were to them, and other men had repeated it. He could almost lay out the exact plan of what was going to happen. After stripping the fort of everything it held, they would gun down the unarmed men. Or maybe the shooting would come first. The order of events had little importance. He felt sick with his futility. Why had they all thrown down their guns? It would have been far better to have resisted. Those four rifles would have taken a price, but they couldn't have gotten all of them before the wolfers were swarmed under by sheer weight of numbers. Quite a few of them would have come out alive; this way none of them would. But all that was hindsight and completely worthless. If a single man had made a break, he would have pulled the others along. But each man had probably felt as Brent had, that a rifle was aimed straight at him. No one had wanted to make the first move and have his belly blown open.

He heard the two shots, and Jed came back. The waiting dragged endlessly, and the sun picked up a burning intensity. He suddenly knew a thirst greater than any he had ever experienced, and he knew how useless it would be to ask for water. The man giving orders would treat that with the greatest derision.

He heard the scraping of feet up and down the line as men shifted their positions and wondered if each of them was going through the same mental and physical torture as he was.

He heard a common sucking in of breath that denoted surprise. He turned his head and saw Haines coming out of his blacksmith shop a dozen yards away.

"What the hell's going on?" he asked.

Culver's face was slack with astonishment. "Where did he come from?"

Hampton's face was torn apart by a new fear. My God! He had forgotten about Haines. At times Haines became so engrossed in working with his metals that he didn't hear a man come up right behind him.

Hampton spoke in desperate haste. "He's hard of hearing."

"You didn't call him out," Culver roared, and swung the back of his hand into Hampton's face. The blow knocked him down, and he lay looking at the big man with swimming eyes.

Culver turned his head toward Haines. "Get in line, you bastard."

Brent saw something that put a tic in his cheek. Haines was holding the tongs in his leather-gloved hand. They must have been in the fire for some time, for they were white hot. He jerked his head at Haines, a barely perceptible movement, and prayed that Haines would see it.

Haines did. He came down the line and wedged in between Brent and Daggett. The hand holding the tongs was next to Brent.

"Cover me," Brent whispered.

He drew a deep breath, then snatched the tongs from Haines. The handle burned his palm, and he set his teeth against its bite. As he stepped quickly back, Haines and Daggett closed, hiding him. He ran at a crouch, heading for the powder room.

"Stop that man," Culver screamed.

A bullet thwocked into the log wall beside the door as Brent darted through it. That keg of opened powder had to be there. He wouldn't have time to open another one.

He gasped in relief as he saw it. He heard hard, slamming steps, then the light was blocked out in the doorway.

His harsh breathing made his voice unsteady. "Hold it right there. This is powder. Make another move, and I'll blow you to pieces." He held the hot tongs just above the powder. "Pull that trigger, and I'll drop the tongs into the keg."

Culver could see that it was powder. Brent saw the indecision in his face, the grappling with this sudden change.

The tongs would be cooling, and he prayed not too much. "You think they're not hot enough." If he couldn't prove they were, he was lost; but he took the chance. He moved the tongs to the side of the keg, and a thin curl of smoke edged upward from the wood.

Culver had a few seconds then, but he didn't take advantage of them. His bulging eyes seemed mesmerized by the hot tongs.

Brent quickly placed them back over the powder. "Did you ever see a man blown up by powder? It scatters his blood and guts all over the place until a buzzard has to hunt to find anything. When this keg goes, the rest stacked behind it will go too. All that will be left of this fort and everybody in it will be a hole in the ground. I'm giving you twenty seconds to get off this post."

"You'd blow yourself up too" That was the voice of a terror-stricken man.

Brent gave him a mirthless grin. "If a man's got to die, the way doesn't make a hell of a lot of difference. One, two . . ."

He made his counting slow and measured. Culver broke at the count of five. He wheeled and ran outside, yelling in wild terror, "Get out of here. Get out. He's going to blow up the place."

It seemed an eternity before Brent heard the rapid roll of hoofbeats. He stepped to the door, still carrying the tongs. The pain from his burned palm filled his arm, making it numb. He dropped the tongs, and they smoked sullenly in contact with the ground.

The four horses were streaming through the gate, and Brent dared look at his hand. It was fiery red and beginning to swell. He lifted his eyes. Everybody seemed frozen to the spot and incapable of thinking.

110

"Get that damned gate closed," he screamed.

A half-dozen men ran for the gate, but Daggett had reacted quickest and reached it first. He slammed it shut and barred it, then leaned weakly against it. He wiped his face before he straightened and came back to Brent. Brent held his hand palm up, and Daggett looked at it.

"Jesus Christ," Daggett whispered. "Somebody get something for this hand. Goddam it, move!"

Brent stared vaguely around him. Everything had a sense of unreality, and maybe it was because he hadn't expected to have this time. That's it, he thought shakily. I don't have any right to it.

Hampton was just getting up off the ground, and men were grabbing up rifles and running for the loopholes.

Brent felt suddenly faint and closed his eyes. Wasn't this ridiculous? But if he didn't have something to lean against, he was going to fall. Daggett's arm went about him.

Jed's senses were still scattered. Cass had come racing out of that room yelling something about being blown up. His panic had engulfed the others, and their rout had pulled Jed with them. He admitted he had run from some unknown terror, but now sane thoughts were filtering back into his head.

He urged his horse up even with Cass's. "What went wrong?"

Cass's voice sounded as though it had too much slobber in it. "A crazy man," he panted. "He was going to blow all of us up."

How could one man possibly blow all of them up? But whatever had happened had scared Cass out of his wits.

A rifle cracked from the fort, and Lamar threw up his hands. Jed got a glimpse of his face; it was frozen in a wild set look. Lamar stayed with his horse for a half-dozen more jumps, then slowly tumbled out of the saddle.

Jed heard another report, and Erb went down. Jed bent as low as he could, knowing the next bullet would find him. He cursed Cass Culver. Cass had run—run when there was no need for it.

He lived an eternity while his horse kept running. The rifles kept up a steady popping, and while he couldn't hear the bullets, he knew they were singing about them.

The reports grew fainter, and he dared to take a full breath. They were going to make it.

He heard the labor come into the horses' breathings. The others were racing out of the brush toward them, and Cass waved frantically to turn them and send them back. The two bands merged, and horses were wheeling all around Jed, turning in a different direction.

Cass ran his horse for another five hundred yards before he pulled it up.

Jed slipped to the ground, and his legs were unsteady. Only now was his skin beginning to loosen a little. Men swung down all around him, and the same question was in every face. What happened?

Jed's eyes were bitter. The biggest prize of their lives was in their hands, and Cass had snatched it away from them. It made him sick to think about what he could have done with his share.

His voice was as brittle as an ice-frozen leaf. "Tell us about it, Cass."

Cass's voice was strained and jerky, and his eyes were glassy at a picture he remembered. "He was crazy. He got into the powder room with a pair of red-hot tongs. He held them over an opened barrel of powder. He had enough powder in there to blow that damned fort to hell. Have you ever seen a man blown up that way? His blood and guts get scattered all over."

Every one of them could see him shudder. Cass had been up against something that had scared him senseless.

Cass looked from face to face, and his face flamed. Didn't they believe him?

Jed eased his pistol out while Cass was looking the other way. He was gagging on his bitterness. It was in their hands, and Cass had made them drop it.

"Cass," he said softly.

Cass's head came back to him, and his face went doughy at the sight of the gun in Jed's hand.

"One man turned your blood to water, Cass? You had a rifle. You could've shot him."

Cass threw out a pleading hand. Jed didn't understand. He

112

could have shot the man, but the tongs would have dropped into the keg. He had saved them all, and Jed didn't understand.

"Jed—" The rest of his words were blotted out by the great spurting hole in his throat. His eyes were shocked as he fought to stay erect. A hand raised to the wound, and blood leaked between the fingers. His eyes flamed with a sudden unnatural brightness, and he crumpled slowly.

Jed looked down at him, the bitterness still etching his face. "He took it away from us." He looked from face to face and saw no protest.

Parney always grabbed an opportunity. "I'm damned glad you did it, Jed. You can lead us a hell of a lot better than he did."

It was a new and strange idea, and it took a few seconds to get used to it. But the bobbing heads all around him said nobody disagreed with Parney.

He put the gun away. "Let's go." He turned toward his horse, and Parney tugged at his sleeve.

"What should we do with him, Jed?"

"Leave him where he is. Bring his horse."

He mounted, and the others bunched up behind him. Parney rode up beside him. "Jed, you got any tobacco?"

"Parney, get back there with the rest of them." Parney gaped at him but hauled up his horse.

Jed rode on, satisfaction filling his face. Things had changed. The sooner they learned it, the better it would be for them. And that included Parney.

16

BRENT FOUND himself the man of the hour. He couldn't take a dozen steps without men flocking around him, repeating the same congratulations they had given him an hour before. His back was sore from the pounding it received, and he turned down enough offers of whiskey to last him a solid drinking month. If these men hadn't fully realized before what he had done, Daggett made it plain. It seemed that everyplace he looked, Daggett was talking to a small bunch of men. If he had any doubt he was the subject of the talk, Daggett always dispelled it by gesturing toward him. Hampton wasn't in evidence. He had put a piercing glance on Brent right after the wolfers had disappeared, then wheeled abruptly, strode into his room, and slammed the door. He hadn't been out since. Brent wondered if Hampton was berating himself for the part he had played in this. The man couldn't have done anything else, but the knowledge probably wouldn't make it set any easier.

Daggett was a busy man the rest of the afternoon, and Brent's frown increased. He could tell that Daggett was still talking about him by the way men's eyes swung to him. He wished Daggett would drop it. His hand ached in steady throbbing pulsations, and though the sling let it ride easier, he was still very much aware of the pain. The ointment Daggett had smeared on the burn helped a lot, but only time would take all the fire out of it.

He ate a few bites, but he wasn't hungry. The night was going to be one of noisy celebration. Already, some of the more eager ones had kicked it off. If they expected him to be part of the revelry, they were going to be disappointed.

He came around a corner to find Daggett and four men a few steps ahead. The gathering dusk and their interest in what they were discussing kept them from seeing him at first. He started to retreat, not wanting to be drawn into more congratulations, but Daggett's words caught his attention.

"What else is it but a sellout? I'm telling you Hampton made a deal with them to lead them into the post. You know where we'd be, if Brent hadn't acted?"

Trimble wisely bobbed his head. "In hell."

"You're damned right we would. And I'm saying Hampton will try it again."

"What are we going to do about it, Daggett?"

"Not we. I'll take care of it. I just wanted to see how you felt about it."

Brent pulled back around the corner and waited.

In a few moments Daggett came around the corner whistling. The whistling broke off when he saw Brent. "Brent, boy. I didn't know you were around."

The greeting was false. It showed in Daggett's narrowed

114

eyes. Brent wasted no time in getting to the core. "I heard part of your talk with them."

"You did?" The question was only to buy Daggett a few seconds to think. His eyes were as wary as a lynx's.

"You've been working on them all afternoon, haven't you?"

"Are you fighting me on this, Brent?"

Something was rushing to a head, and Brent had no intention of stepping in between Hampton and Daggett in an effort to stop it. He didn't care that much about either of them.

"I don't like you using me. You keep me out of it from now on."

For a man in his condition those were tough words. He couldn't begin to hold a gun butt.

He heard Daggett's gusty breathing, and it should have put an alarm in him. Daggett's laugh had a harsh, brittle note. "You're not against me, are you, Brent?"

The conversation had turned into safer channels, and Brent's anger dissipated, leaving him only weary. "I just want you to know I'm no part of your quarrel with Hampton."

"Understood." Daggett's voice was easier. "The boys feel the same as I do. Hampton sold us out. He'll do it again."

"I heard," Brent said dryly. With a quick flash of understanding Brent knew why Daggett had been talking to the men. He had to see where he stood before he moved ahead. He had to find out how many would back Hampton, how much opposition he faced.

"They all agree with you, don't they, Daggett?"

Daggett's nod held wicked satisfaction. "They do. I'm not doing this for me, Brent. I'm doing it for them."

Daggett was a liar, and Brent almost said it. He saw the hard assurance that firmed Daggett's face, and thought, Tonight. He's going to end it tonight. Should he warn Hampton? He entertained that question for only a second or two. He owed Hampton nothing, and he had no particular love for him. If he managed to stop it tonight, he merely delayed it. This quarrel had ancient roots, and Daggett had never forgotten them.

Daggett drew a deep breath. "I'm going to take over the

post, Brent. And I won't be forgetting what you did for me."

That must be sticking big in the man's head. Daggett had his own peculiar kind of loyalty.

"Sure," he said, and turned away.

He had intended going to his room, but found he couldn't. The ending of this drew him with a morbid fascination. He was in the compound, near Hampton's room, when Daggett approached it.

"Hampton," Daggett bellowed. "Come out here. I want to talk to you."

Every man within hearing rushed to the scene. All of them seemed to know what was going to happen. Maybe Daggett had told them, or maybe they smelled it. The prospect of spilled blood drew as many people as flies.

"Goddam it, Hampton," Daggett roared, "do I have to come in after you?"

The silence was long and strained. Hampton must have known from Daggett's tone what that talk was going to be. He could duck it by remaining in a locked room. But he had to know that wouldn't save him.

The door opened, and Hampton stepped onto the compound. He had buckled on a gunbelt, and it looked grotesque under his sagging belly. He moved slowly, as though each step was a painful effort, and the poor illumination from nearby lanterns cast a weird light on his pallid face.

He knows, Brent thought. He knows. It took a lot of guts for Hampton to come out here. He must have made some kind of peace with the coming moment.

"Start it, Daggett." His voice was quite steady.

That steadiness upset Daggett. It was something he hadn't figured on. Brent, standing off to one side, could see the unsureness wash his face.

"You made a deal with the wolfers. You sold us out."

A low murmur of approval arose from either side of him.

"Ah." Hampton caught it in quick understanding. "You've convinced all of them of that. You're a liar, Daggett. You know it, and I know it. And when they know you a little longer, they'll know it."

Why, Brent thought in amazement, he's not afraid. He was

116

sure that at one time he had seen fear of Daggett in Hampton. But it was gone now, burned away in some crucible that only Hampton knew about.

Emotion twitched across Daggett's face again, and Brent wondered if a fear of Hampton was growing in him. It could possibly be, for Hampton was taking this far differently than Daggett had expected, or anybody else for that matter. But if Daggett did know a touch of fear, it wouldn't change the ultimate outcome, for Daggett had more skill and speed in his favor.

Brent studied Hampton's face. The paleness was still there but nothing else. No quivering, no sagging. I think he knows this is Daggett's minute, Brent thought. And he doesn't give a damn. Maybe that was where Hampton got his strength.

"Are you worried, Daggett?" The low words carried a mocking edge. "You pushed it to this point, and now you're not quite sure. Wouldn't it be a funny thing if you couldn't handle it?"

Sweat glistened on Daggett's face. It would be a hell of a funny thing, but nobody would be laughing. Daggett was a fool. The longer he prolonged this, the more it would fray his nerves. Hampton handled words too well. He put little rat teeth in them that ate at Daggett's mind.

"Shut up, you fat bastard," and there was a crack in Daggett's voice. He dug for his gun, and a seasoned gunman would have noticed the raggedness in his movement. A seasoned gunman would have cut him down where he stood, but Hampton wasn't that. He expelled a breath, and it whipped through his nostrils as he slapped at the gunbutt. He let the desperate need for haste overpower him, and it made his draw jerky. His gun was barely out of the holster when Daggett shot him.

The bullet took him in the chest, and its numbing power showed in the way it slammed him back a step. The intensity of the effort to hold on to the gun showed in his face, turning it into an agonized mask. His fingers weakened, and he dropped the gun. He slewed around in a half circle and fell. He rolled over onto his back, and one hand tried to plug the gushing hole.

He looked directly at Brent, and his eyes were blazing.

"You still picked the wrong man, Brent." The face went rigid in that final set.

It shook Brent hard. Nobody would have ever picked Hampton for a brave man. But from the moment he had appeared in his doorway, he had been filled with bravery.

It shook Daggett, too, for he slurred his words. "Well, get the bastard buried, and I'll buy everybody a drink."

They crowded around him, seeking standing with this new authority.

Daggett looked over at Brent. "You coming?"

"No." Brent made no effort to soften the word. He twisted on his heel. With every step he expected to hear Daggett yell at him.

Daggett came to his room in the morning. The ravages in his face said he had celebrated hard last night. The edginess of anger was in his eyes. "You against me, Brent?" He was trying to find out on what ground he stood.

God, yes, Brent was against him. "No." The word gave Daggett no help.

"I didn't know Hampton meant that much to you."

"He didn't mean a damned thing to me."

Relief was in Daggett's sigh. "I thought you'd like to ride over with me to see Macleod." At Brent's frown he explained. "You haven't forgotten about what I told you I'd do with this place if I ever had it? And I promised you a cut if I ever sold it."

Brent could have hooted with derisive laughter. That offer was for then. Time and conditions had changed it. Yes, he wanted to ride over with Daggett. He wanted to see his face when Macleod told him what a fool he was.

Most of the trip was covered in silence. Once, Daggett asked how the hand was, and Brent grunted a "Fine." It wasn't fine; it still throbbed like hell. If there was a lessening in its hurting, it was too small to find.

His silence must have grated on Daggett's nerves, for as they came in sight of the Mounties' post, he said, "By God, you're a hard man to know."

Brent gave him a bleak grin. "Yes."

He was amazed to see how far the building of Fort Macleod had progressed. A great deal of work remained to be done, but much of the fort was already livable. He wondered if Daggett was contrasting the appearance of this post with that of Whoop-up and decided he wasn't. The cleanliness and orderliness would make no impression on him.

Daggett's face was flushed, and his eyes were shining. Brent thought sardonically, He's already counting his money.

Two troopers held them at the gate while another went for the major. Brent looked at the alert, hard-eyed men. They're tough, he thought.

Macleod strode briskly toward them. His greeting was barely civil. "What do you want?"

Daggett started to dismount, and Macleod stopped him. "That won't be necessary. Our business won't take that long."

That put a different kind of flush in Daggett's face. "You'll change your tune, Major, when you learn why I'm here. I can sell you Whoop-up. I can be ready to move out on a day's notice."

Macleod gave him a pitying smile. "Will you tell me what I would do with two forts?"

It put a sick confusion in Daggett's face. The ride was worthwhile to Brent just to see it.

"You mean you don't want Whoop-up now?"

Macleod must have been enjoying Daggett's misery, for his eyes had a hard gleam in them. "I've got a fort, mister. My offer was good as long as I didn't have one." His voice and face hardened. "I'll give you the advice I gave Hampton. Close your fort, mister, before I have to close it for you. You won't like that closing."

Daggett's face flowed alternately red and white. "You come after us. You come after us any damned time you please."

He jerked his horse around and set spurs into it. When Brent caught up with him, Daggett was a madman. "Let him come after us," he raved. "Let him go up against our walls. We'll pick them off like sitting ducks."

"He won't make that kind of a mistake." Brent knew it as surely as though Macleod had told him so. "I saw two cannon in there. Bigger than ours. He can just sit back and knock holes in your walls." Some of his despondency at his failure was leaving him. If he waited a little longer, he might be able to take back a report to Moore that Whoop-up no longer existed. It wouldn't be what Moore wanted, but it would be something. But he had better make certain about one thing. He had better be out of Whoop-up when Macleod came.

He listened to Daggett's swearing until it ran down. "What are you going to do with Whoop-up now?"

He saw that Daggett changed his mind about what he was going to say. Evidently, the idea had just hit him. "Why, I'll run it. Give me three or four good trades, and I'll take enough out of it." Despite his cursing at Macleod, the man worried him. "Then Macleod can have it."

Brent only half listened to Daggett formulate further plans. Yes, Daggett might make himself some money out of a few more trading days; that is, if Macleod gave him the time.

17

THE TROOPER found Macleod inspecting the off foreleg of a bay horse. "It's coming along nicely, Larry," Macleod said. "For a while I was afraid we might lose him." He touched the man's shoulder. "You've got a way with horses."

Larry beamed his pleasure. "Thank you, sir."

The trooper waited until Macleod was turning away. "We thought you might want to see this, sir. Lieutenant Samson is bringing in two wagons and a dozen men."

Macleod frowned. "He's escorting a trading party here?"

"They look more like prisoners, sir."

Macleod's frown deepened. Now what the hell had happened that authorized the taking of prisoners?

He was waiting at the gate when Samson arrived. His eyes took in the wagons, piled high with robes and furs, then flicked to the prisoners. He could search Canada over and never find a more sullen-looking bunch of rogues.

"What is this?" he snapped.

"Whiskey traders, sir," Samson answered. "We found them

just breaking up camp. They had been trading with a small bunch of Piegans. The Indians were helplessly drunk. These men were making their getaway while they could. I thought you would like to talk to them."

"We aren't ready for this yet, Lieutenant. The post isn't finished. I sent you out as a hunting party."

Samson's eyes danced. "I know, sir, but the men and I talked it over. We didn't think it would do any harm to mix a little pleasure with business."

Macleod almost allowed his smile to show. "You know, you may be right." He stepped to the nearest prisoner. "What's your name?"

The man's face was insolent, and for a moment Macleod didn't think he was going to answer, but he must have read something in the major's eyes that advised him to change his mind. "Quade," he said sullenly. "You can't arrest us. We're American citizens. Wait until our government hears about this."

"You're trespassing on Canadian soil while engaged in illegal business, breaking your country's and my country's laws."

Quade smirked. "Turn us over to American authority. We're willing to stand on what they say."

Macleod eyed him thoughtfully. "You'd like that, wouldn't you? No, it's too far for us to ride to escort you there. We'll do your government a favor and take you off their hands." He turned to Samson. "Bring them to the officers' mess."

The tables were shoved back when the prisoners entered the room. Their eyes were apprehensive, but Quade was still belligerent. "You can't hold us," he bawled. "By God, the army will come after us."

Macleod smashed his fist on the table before him. "Hold your tongue. From now on, you'll speak when you're spoken to. Do you understand that?"

Quade failed to meet his eyes. "Yes," he mumbled.

Macleod's officers acted as prosecutors, judges, and jury. Twelve pairs of eyes touched those rock-carved faces and moved uneasily away.

"Lieutenant, state your evidence."

"We found three dozen bottles of whiskey that hadn't been

traded. Empties were all over the place. We dumped the bottles, sir."

"You retained none of it as evidence?" Macleod's tone was sharp. There was a proper way of doing these things.

A smile flickered on Samson's face. "We brought in a bottle, sir." He pulled it out of his pocket and uncorked it. "I knew you would want it." He stepped forward and handed the bottle to Macleod.

Again that smile almost broke out. Smug young pup. But he was going to make a good man.

Macleod sniffed at the bottle neck and grimaced at the rank smell. Trade whiskey, all right. How could men put such hog swill into their stomachs? He handed the bottle to the other four officers who were sitting with him as judges. Each man smelled the bottle and made the same grimace.

"Gentlemen?" he asked.

Four heads bobbed together, and each answer was the same. "Trade whiskey, sir."

Macleod's eyes blazed at Quade. "I know you don't give a damn for the misery you brought into this country. But maybe we can teach you to care. Guilty of illegal trading. Your horses, wagons, guns you brought in, and all goods you took in in trading are confiscated. Each of you is sentenced to a two-hundred-dollar fine ... or six months in jail." He cursed himself. In his hurry to get the sentence out, he had forgotten to poll the other judges, but their faces said they were in full agreement with him.

He saw varying degrees of stupefaction on the prisoners' faces as each reacted to the shock according to his nature. It took Quade a long time to recover. "You can't do that," he bawled. "I'm an American citizen. I demand—"

"The sentence is double for Mr. Quade. Do any of the rest wish to protest their sentences?"

Tongues licked lips gone suddenly dry, and not a one of them opened his mouth.

"Good! You will pay your fines or be taken to jail."

By pooling their money, the traders raised enough to pay one fine. It couldn't be Quade's, for his fine had been doubled.

Quade picked one of the younger men, a weak-faced, bad-skinned man in his early twenties. "Bob, you get back to

Benton as fast as you can and tell everybody what's happened to us." He turned his head toward Macleod. "He gets his horse back, don't he?"

Macleod nodded gravely.

"Git going, Bob." Quade waited until he was out of the room, and his face filled with triumph. "You didn't know who he was, did you?"

Macleod showed no interest.

"He's the son of one of the leading merchants. Wait until that man gets through raising hell about this."

Now Macleod's interest was aroused. "This man's money backed you, didn't it?"

The reason for the question puzzled Quade, but he finally said, "Yes. He's a big man. He can raise a private army to come after us. He—" He stopped and stared in awe at the rage sweeping Macleod's face.

"I hope he does come. I hope he's joined by every illicit backer of the whiskey trade. If I could only get them on Canadian soil—" Macleod drew a deep breath and controlled himself. "Do you think it's your kind I'm chiefly interested in? You're only the surface scum. It's the deep-down filth I want to clean away." He had something else he wanted to say, and he abruptly closed his mouth. "Take them away," he said wearily.

Samson hesitated, and Macleod asked, "What is it?"

"Sir, I was just thinking, one wall of the jail isn't finished."

Macleod's eyes had a wicked glint of humor. "Ah, so you remembered it, did you? How long do you estimate it will take to finish it?"

"Two or three days, sir."

"Then the prisoners are your responsibility for that period. I would hate to have to think about you losing any of them."

Samson didn't make a sound, but just the same the groan was there.

Macleod smiled as Samson marched the prisoners out of the room. Samson wouldn't dare sleep until that jail was finished. It wouldn't hurt him at all; it could even be beneficial. It might dampen down his ardor. He snorted. Bringing in prisoners before they were ready to handle them! But dealing with the traders had given him pure pleasure. He would have to find out where those Piegan were and get those robes and furs back to them. The confiscated horses weren't too much. Maybe he would give those to the Piegans, too. Yes, it all left a good taste in his mouth, and he could thank Samson for that. He guessed Samson had a very potent idea. He should mix pleasure with business more often. A few more arrests, and word-of-mouth would spread it rapidly that the redcoats meant business. The faster the word spread, the less work they would have to do. It could put enough fear into the whiskey traders to develop into a regular exodus out of Canada. He would give several months' pay to see that.

His eyes glistened as he thought that tomorrow wouldn't be too soon to start. But looking for the small individual traders would be a hit-or-miss business, and they would like as not find more failure than success. But the established posts, those were fixed, and they could ride up to them any time they chose. Whoop-up was by far the largest, but there were Stand-off and Slide-out, both much smaller posts. It might be wiser to pick one of the smaller ones first. Give everybody experience on how to handle these posts, including himself. He pulled at his lower lip. Might be a smart idea to take one of the cannon along. If the whiskey traders proved stubborn, a couple of holes in their walls would change their minds.

He sat there smiling with satisfaction. It wouldn't hurt to put off the start until the jail was finished. Samson had certainly earned the right to be in on this expedition. And he had to be left on guard duty until that wall was built. Bad for discipline if he wasn't. His smile grew. He could see the delight in Samson's eyes when he told him.

18

How MANY times had Brent looked toward the west in the last few weeks? He might as well face it: Macleod had made a lot of talk, but that was all it was. Talk with nothing to back it up. The Mounties had no intention of riding against Whoop-up. He guessed its size was too formidable.

But there had been a report that Macleod had taken Fort Stand-off and burned it. As yet the report was unconfirmed. Brent decided it was a lying rumor.

Things were going badly here. Daggett had no head for detail, and if possible, Whoop-up was more dirty and disorderly than when Hampton ran it. Some inner anxiety seemed to be spurring Daggett every minute. He rarely spoke in less than a bellow anymore, and he would issue an order one minute and countermand it the next. He used his fists and feet too often, and last week he had killed a man for no ready reason.

Two men had slipped away from the post the previous night, and under the kind of pressure Daggett was using, the desertions would come faster.

Brent heard him now, screaming at the top of his lungs. It had to be some kind of fear that put that much tension in a man, and Brent wondered which particular kind it was in Daggett. Was it fear of the big man back in Benton? He had considered that, and it could readily be. The last three trades had been bad, but even so, Daggett hadn't sent anything back to Benton. Whoever was backing Whoop-up was surely beginning to wonder why no loaded wagons were rolling back to Benton. After wonder would come investigation, and then Daggett's string would snap. Yes, Brent decided, that had to be the cause of Daggett's tension. He would feel the same if he was in Daggett's shoes. It always drove a man crazy not knowing how much time he had left to do a certain thing.

Brent thought back over the last three trades. Daggett couldn't get things organized the way Hampton had. The more he ran around yelling orders, the more he tangled things. He had been impatient to get the trading started, and he had eliminated the ceremonial rites so dear to the Indian heart. One tribe had ridden away without trading at all, and for the Indians to turn down a chance at whiskey showed how offended they were.

Tomorrow the Blackfeet were coming in, the same bunch of Blackfeet Brent had seen in the first trading here. He couldn't possibly see how the trading could be any good. Those Blackfeet hadn't had time enough to accumulate anything worthwhile.

Daggett came to Brent's room that night. Even sitting down,

he seemed as though he was ready to jump at the slightest sound. He rolled a cigarette and handed the sack to Brent. "I'm not doing very well, am I?" His teeth bared in a painful grin.

Brent shrugged. Daggett had said it, but he would fly at the throat of any man who agreed with him.

Daggett didn't seal his cigarette properly, and it fell apart in his hand. Brent expected him to fly into a rage. Instead, he sat staring at the ruined cigarette, then dropped it to the floor. His grin seemed even more painful. "I've been doing some thinking, Brent. I think I know my trouble. I've been hurrying things too much. Hampton got a lot out of the Indians because he was patient with them. Maybe it's about time I learned something."

"Sure." The word neither encouraged nor discouraged.

The restlessness pushed Daggett to his feet. "Watch me tomorrow. I'll get everything they've got."

He stayed a few minutes longer, then left. Thoughts kept crowding sleep from Brent's mind. Daggett had been doing some self-analysis. Maybe his remaining time was enough; maybe he could still pull out of the fire whatever purpose he had in mind.

Brent thought he remembered some of the Indians who rode up to the gate. They were still the same impassive faces, but he couldn't help but wonder what resentments lurked in the smokey depths of their eyes. Their clothing wasn't good, and he would say they had walked in hard times. It couldn't be possible they had forgotten what put them in those times.

Daggett admitted the chieftains, and he was lavish in his attention. Instead of the free drink Hampton had given them, he gave them three. The liquor loosened them up, and the laughter and speech-making seemed to run on forever.

He watched them ride back to their camp, and his face was triumphant. "They'll come back with everything they have."

He stood at the wicket, waiting for them to return, and his hands couldn't be still. They showed the impatience that burned within him.

Fury flashed in his eyes as he saw the scantily burdened

horses. And it grew as the Indians pushed the first of the robes and furs through the wicket. They were of poor quality, and at best, would bring a cut rate. The few bottles already given the Indians were having their effect, and some of them were dancing and howling with drunken laughter.

A brave pushed a moth-eaten robe through the wicket. It was greasy and stiff with use, and great patches of fur had fallen out of it. Brent saw Daggett's chest swell with rage as he shoved it back.

"Get out of here," he snapped with startling suddenness. "Get out of here."

The Indian stood grinning foolishly, trying to shove the robe back to Daggett.

Daggett's last restraint was gone. He grabbed up a rifle and pumped a bullet into the Indian's chest. The man clutched his chest, staring at Daggett with eyes filled with shock and disbelief. Then he slumped to the ground.

"Goddammit. Didn't I tell you to leave?" Daggett babbled like a hysterical woman. He worked the lever as fast as his hand could move, and aiming through the wicket, emptied the magazine.

The Indians were frozen, and at this close range Daggett couldn't miss. When the magazine was emptied, five more Blackfeet lay on the ground.

Brent had been chained in that same nightmare of horror. He threw it off and sprang forward. With one hand he jerked the rifle away, with the other he slammed Daggett on the jaw hinge. Daggett went down as though he had been axed.

The Indians were fleeing in wild disorder, leaving their dead.

Brent cursed in futility. He came very close to pulling his gun and pumping a bullet into Daggett. He looked at the other faces, and the same mold of shock had seized them.

"Throw him in his room," he ordered. "Grab up your rifles." The Blackfeet had every right to try to stamp out this place.

They waited several tight hours and saw not a sign of an Indian. But they would come, if not tonight or tomorrow, sometime in the future.

"He's crazy, isn't he?" Haines asked, his eyes worried.

"Yes."

Haines' face turned bitter. "He did it. But they'll blame every one of us. We'll be on watch all night."

They would, and each tense hour would build a greater hate for Daggett.

Brent saw Daggett for a brief period at nightfall. He came out of his room, his face looking as though it were carved out of rock. When he returned, he clutched a bottle in his fist.

Drink your damned head off, Brent thought. Drown yourself in it. You'd be better off.

Night minutes passed far more slowly than day minutes. He judged it was near midnight when somebody farther down the walkway hissed, "I hear something."

Brent saw the dark bent forms approaching the walls. Something in the way they moved told him this was no war party. "Hold your fire," he ordered. "They can't get over the walls." There had been too much killing already.

The forms crept up to the dead figures, and Brent had the impression fearful faces were turned upwards to them. "They're trying to collect their dead. Let them alone."

The rustling noise outside the wall continued for a long while, then diminished. The dead figures were no longer in front of the gate.

"Keep your watch," he said. But he didn't think the Indians would be back that night. In that far bunch of lodges there would be much wailing and the swearing of savage vows. Right now, one was as ineffectual as the other in erasing their loss.

He left the walls to get something to eat, and when he returned, he saw a massing of dark shadows at the gate. Those shadows were bigger than men; they had to be horses.

He made no attempt to stop them. He counted them as the gate swung open. Eight riders rode through it in file. He didn't have to wait on Macleod. Daggett would kill Whoop-up all by himself.

19

IN THE morning Daggett's face looked like a ruin. He was sick in the head and sick in the belly. He couldn't meet Brent's eyes.

"I lost my head," he mumbled. He tried to stand and almost fell. His stomach heaved, and he grabbed his mouth and ran outside. Brent followed and watched him being sick with a small, wicked satisfaction. He hoped Daggett would puke his insides out.

Daggett's face was drained of color when he finished. He staggered to a wall and leaned against it. "Are the Indians gone?"

"Yes." Brent had ridden out early in the morning. From a good distance off he could see that the lodges were down.

"I'm not sorry." Daggett's defiance slid off his face under Brent's eyes. "What the hell were they? Nothing but dirty Indians. Nobody's lost anything."

"Maybe you lost your hair. How long do you think it will take to spread the word about this? In less than a week you'll have a thousand Indians going against these walls."

Daggett's face drained even whiter.

"That's not all you lost. Eight men deserted last night." Haines was one of them. Maybe they had picked a good time for it. At least they would have a start for the border before any possible Indian uprising could come.

Daggett emptied himself of swearing. "I don't need them. I'll pay the men who stick with me well. We'll strip the fort and load up the wagons."

"You don't think you can take them to Benton, do you? Won't somebody there be looking for you?" He still hoped to hear that name from Daggett.

"Benton's not the only town in Montana," Daggett growled. "Stay with me, Brent. I'll split with you."

He ought to kill him; he ought to kill him right now. Daggett might make it through, and the thought of him profiting from this, even in the smallest degree, sickened Brent.

He knew suddenly what he was going to do. Daggett would get no profit out of them. He was going to take Daggett back to Benton; he was going to tell what he had seen. Moore would see to taking care of the rest.

But there were still men in Whoop-up who might object to his taking Daggett prisoner. All right, he would wait. A few more days wouldn't make any difference. The talk among them would be on nothing but the eight desertions. The desertions had started and would soon grow into a flood. They might all go tonight. He would bet on it that some of them would. And each desertion would only increase the panic until it engulfed them all. Yes, he could afford a few more days to get his hands on Daggett.

"I'll stick."

Daggett gave him a wan grin. "I knew you would. I knew—" He broke it off under those hot eyes.

At the end of the second day they were down to eight men, and nerves twanged like plucked violin strings. It wasn't safe to come up on a man unexpectedly. They all jumped at the slightest sound, and eyes shifted fearfully.

It was slow work loading the wagons with this small force. Daggett kept four men on the walls, watching for signs of Indians while the others labored. Six wagons were loaded, and the men wanted to leave that night.

Daggett argued against it. "Four more wagons is all I want. That's a wagon for each of us. And that wagon belongs to the driver. We can leave by noon tomorrow."

The appeal to their greed held them. But there was something sly in Daggett's eyes. Brent didn't know what he had in mind, but he was sure it was nothing good for the rest of them. Daggett wouldn't be able to handle those wagons by himself. He would let them drive the wagons as far as the border, then there would be nine dead men. And that number includes me, Brent finished grimly.

He thought about warning the others, then decided to wait. Staying together as long as possible might be the best way of getting Daggett across the border.

He awakened in the morning, and the sun was barely up. But already Daggett was bellowing orders to get those damned wagons loaded. He stepped outside and yawned. The moment he drove out of that gate, he would be matching wits with Daggett. And the first time he allowed his attention to get a little sloppy could be his last.

"Daggett!" Trimble was gesticulating like a crazy man, stabbing out a forefinger repeatedly. "They're all around us." His voice rose higher and higher until it was a scream. "Hundreds of them."

Brent's heart stuck in his throat. They had waited a night too long.

Daggett's face was ashen. "Who is it?"

Trimble acted as though he hadn't heard the question. He just kept pointing over and over. Or maybe what he saw froze his tongue.

Daggett cursed him as he ran toward a ladder. Brent pounded at his heels. His thoughts were stuck in the molasses of his mind, and he couldn't get them unstuck.

He climbed the ladder after Daggett, and for an instant he thought the horizon was aflame. Then he understood why he thought so. The morning sun struck fully on the Mounties' redcoats. The thin red line stretched clear across in front of the fort and bent at either end. There was no need to look in other directions. Brent knew that red line went clear around Whoop-up. Trimble was wrong in saying there were hundreds of them. Maybe a hundred and half of another. It was more than enough.

Trimble's tongue seemed to be able to move again. "Rider coming in. Carrying a white flag."

Brent could see. The man rode at an unworried pace, pointing a rifle with a white rag or handkerchief tied to its muzzle straight up in the air.

Brent had a hard time hiding his delight. Macleod had come in time.

"I'll show them how I talk," Daggett yelled.

Brent sprant toward him. He struck the rifle down before Daggett had it snugged against his shoulder. "You goddamned fool. He'll blow every stick of this wall down. And us with it."

He thought their struggle was going to pull them off the walkway, then Daggett said, "Let go of me. I'm all right."

Brent dubiously relaxed his hold. Daggett didn't look all

right. If that wasn't madness in his eyes, it as too close to it.

The rider stopped before the gate and lifted his face to them. "Major Macleod orders the immediate surrender of this fort."

"Tell your goddamned major to go to hell," Daggett bawled.

"It's your decision," the Mountie said crisply, and wheeled his horse.

That was madness in Daggett's eyes, Brent decided. The other faces were scared. They knew ten men couldn't hold off that force out there. Daggett would rave and swear, but he would be helpless if the rest of them simply refused to fight.

He was watching the rider move away, and he didn't see Daggett hurry down the walkway to the cannon's platform. He jerked his head around as Daggett yelled, "Take this answer back to him."

Daggett touched a match to the fuse before anybody could do more than think about stopping him. The cannon boomed out its flat, heavy report, and smoke coughed up from is muzzle.

Daggett's aim was bad. The ball gouged a crater almost a hundred yards from the rider. The rider threw his head toward it and continued on his unhurried pace.

Brent raced down the walkway. Daggett was feverishly reloading. Brent reached him as Daggett straightened. He swung with all the violence in him, and the blow landed on Daggett's chin, sweeping him off of the platform. He landed on his back below it. The fall should have broken his neck, and Brent hoped it had.

Macleod had more powerful and longer-range cannon than the one Daggett had just fired. And the retaliation would be quick.

"Get off the walls," Brent yelled at the staring men. "And up against them. Move, damn it. Do you want to be blown to bits?"

He cowered against the base of the wall with the rest of them. Being shot at with a cannon put a horrible weakness in a man's middle.

He heard the oncoming ball, and it had a heavy, sighing

sound like a strengthening wind. That cannoneer's aim was good. The shell landed in the middle of the compound, squarely in the bed of a wagon. Brent's ears ached with its blast, but above that ache was a higher, shriller din, the sound of a horse in agony.

The round caused awesome damage. The remains of the wagon couldn't be identified as such, and the shreds of it were scattered all over the crater in the ground. Some of those shreds weren't wooden, and those showed a glistening wetness. The raw, rank smell of horse manure filled the nose. The other horse had been almost blown in two. How it could go on making those terrible sounds was a mystery.

Brent looked away from the gruesome mess. Another round would be coming in in a few seconds. The gunner was zeroed in. This time it could easily be human flesh shredded like that horse flesh was.

"Get back up there and wave anything that's white." That didn't sound like Brent's voice at all. It was too high and frightened.

All up and down the walkway pieces of white waved. Some of them were bits of rag, a couple of handkerchiefs were so dirty that their original color was almost lost, and one man even waved a square of red.

Brent extended the rifle as high as he could in the air, holding his breath as he waved. Did Macleod see it? Would he pay any attention to it?

He felt limp and drained as the red line slowly began to move forward. "Go down and open the gate," he told Trimble. His voice sounded normal again. It was amazing how a few strained moments could put so much heaviness into a man's feet. If he had been going up the ladder instead of down, he doubted he could have lifted his feet. As he moved toward the gate, he noticed that Daggett was sitting up. The man had a vacant look on his face, but he was feeling of himself, and he didn't seem too badly hurt. That was good. Brent wanted to deliver him to Macleod in as good a shape as he could.

Apparently Macleod felt no trickery was involved, for the long horizontal line pulled in and became a file of twos. Macleod rode at the head of it, and those faces were as unconcerned as though they were on parade.

Brent stepped forward to meet him. "Major, I'm Brent Bargen."

Those keen eyes pierced him. "Are you in charge?"

"No, sir." Brent wasn't aware of the title of respect. "You'll find Daggett inside."

Those eyes didn't soften. "You're the man who made the trip to our post with him?"

Brent nodded.

"How many more men?"

"Eight, Major."

Macleod turned his head to issue an order. "Put the ten men in this post under guard. I'll want them in a few minutes."

Brent hid a furtive grin. Macleod didn't know who he was. The moment he had a few minutes alone with him and explained, the order for his arrest would be revoked. The major might be surprised, but Daggett would be shocked.

Macleod wasted no time. In fifteen minutes the trials began. Brent looked soberly at the stern faces behind the long table. He would hate to be seriously on trial before them.

The court found eight men guilty of engaging in illicit whiskey trading. Macleod stared at each man in turn. "Your weapons, horses, and anything else you have will be confiscated. Two hundred dollars fine each, or six months in jail."

Eight faces were vacant with stunned stupidity. They couldn't come close to raising two hundred dollars between them.

"Take them to Fort Macleod." Macleod seemed lost in thought for a moment. "Bring the other two prisoners forward."

Daggett's face was set in a worried scowl, and an edge of anxiety gnawed on Brent. Why were they being tried separately? He took a step toward Macleod. "Major, could I speak to you alone for a minute?"

"No," Macleod snapped. "And the prisoner will step back."

Brent felt no real worry as yet. But he fretted a little. He wished he could get this cleared up with Macleod.

The evidence took only a few minutes to present. Five

heads bent together and conferred in low voices, then Macleod's head raised.

He looked straight at Daggett. "You were the leader here." He looked at Brent. "And you were second in command."

Brent's throat began pinching him. This was too damned realistic; he felt as though he was actually being tried.

"You two were chiefly responsible." That remorseless voice hammered at them. "For your crimes I sentence you to be hanged in the morning. Take them away and place them under separate guard from the others."

Two troopers put their hands on Brent's arms. He threw them off, and his voice had the near proportions of a shout. "I've got something to say. You've got to listen to me."

He tried to reach the major, and the Mounties grabbed him. Macleod flicked him with cold eyes. "Take that man away."

Brent tried to throw off the hands again, and fingers bit deeper. "Dammit." Now his voice was a shout. "You will listen to me."

He threw the two men about in his struggles, and two more sprang forward to subdue him. They smothered his efforts by sheer weight of numbers.

Macleod's face didn't change. "Get that man out of here," he snapped.

Brent was dragged out of the room, struggling and kicking. He fought them all the way to the supply room. They shoved him into it, and the door slammed behind him. He recovered his balance and whirled, hearing the rasp of a key in the lock. He hammered on the door; he shouted until his voice was scratchy, and he couldn't raise the smallest response.

The one small window set high in the wall gave a poor light. Brent ran his eyes over it and forgot about it. He could never get through it. The walls were built of solid logs. He went out through the door, or he didn't go out.

Daggett sat on a sack of grain, his face white. His eyes couldn't seem to fix on anything, and he kept licking his lips. He had a right to his worry. He had earned every minute of it. But with Brent it was different, entirely different. He was doing a little sweating himself, and it shouldn't have to be.

But up to now it had been too real, and if he didn't keep thinking every minute, panic would wash over him. There was no reason for panic. Time hadn't run out on him. Somewhere in the stretch of hours until tomorrow morning he would find a way to make Macleod listen to him.

He sat down across from Daggett, and he still breathed hard. Daggett enjoyed his agitation; it took his mind off of his own plight. "You cry pretty hard," he jeered.

Brent's muscles bunched, and he forced himself to sit still. Fighting Daggett now wouldn't gain him anything.

Daggett pounded away at him. "Do you like it better this way? You stopped me from fighting them."

"Shut up," Brent yelled. "And keep your damned mouth closed."

Maybe he should have let Daggett go on talking. His laughter was worse.

20

THE LIGHT coming through the tiny window faded, and the room darkened. Daggett paced back and forth; he must have walked twenty miles. He kept up a steady stream of invective. When he wasn't cursing Macleod, he was cursing the inhumanity of not even being given tobacco or a drink. His nerves were fraying thin. It showed in his manner and voice.

Brent was in little better shape. He just wasn't letting it show—yet. The last word echoed ominously in his mind. A good chunk of his time had already been chewed up, and he hadn't improved his position in the least. He brushed by Daggett as he moved to the door and restrained the impulse to shove him violently out of the way.

Some miscellaneous tools were piled in a corner, and he fumbled among them. He wanted an ax to work on that door with, and he couldn't find one. He discarded the shovels as being useless for his purpose. A couple of lusty blows would break the handles off of them. In the darkness his hand closed on a short-handled maul. He might not break down the door with it, but he could draw attention. When he got that, somebody was going to listen to him.

He hammered until he was breathless. His fingers ran over the door's surface. It was a stout one. He found some deep dents in it but nothing that felt like a split in the wood.

He caught his breath and started hammering again.

"Stop that," a voice ordered from the other side.

"Open this door." Brent hit it another lick.

"Stand back from it," the voice ordered.

The door opened cautiously, and the light was good enough for Brent to see the Mountie standing there with leveled rifle.

"What do you want?"

"I have to see Major Macleod. I have important news for him. He's got to listen to it."

The man threw off his indecision. "I'll tell him. But he doesn't like to be disturbed." He shut the door and locked it.

Brent found himself pacing as Daggett had. But he couldn't just stand and wait. My God, what was taking that Mountie so long to deliver a simple message?

He started eagerly as he heard the scratch of the key. The Mountie was coming to escort him to Macleod.

The door swung open, and that rifle was as alert as it had ever been. The rising dismay tightened Brent's throat. "Isn't he going to talk to me?"

"The Major says you have nothing to say that will interest him. If you keep pounding on that door, he says to put a bullet in your leg."

For a moment Brent couldn't speak against the swelling bitterness. The stiff-necked, red-coated bastard. "You tell him I'm not a—"

The door was closing in his face, and he thrust a foot forward to stop it.

"I'm not to listen to anything you say. He said you would think of one lie after another to keep from hanging."

Brent felt something closing in about him. He couldn't see it, but he could feel its clammy touch. He couldn't let that door be closed and locked again, for it was very probably it wouldn't open again until morning. His thoughts raced frantically about like trapped mice. He had to find a way to get this door opened before then.

"Aren't you even going to feed us?" He cursed the quavering in his voice. He wanted to scream at the man; he wanted to scream against everything.

The Mountie shook his head. "How in the hell you can eat now—" He shook his head and didn't finish it. "I'll bring you something."

He dropped the rifle butt on Brent's foot, and as Brent yelped and jerked it back, he slammed the door.

Brent hobbled on his aching foot. The bastards, the dirty bastards. He knew now it would be no different in the morning; nobody was going to listen to him.

Now the panic was a swift-rising tide, threatening to carry him along with it. He had to think, and how could he with tomorrow staring him in the face? He wanted to grab up the maul again, and that would only earn him a bullet in the leg. He twisted a new thought around in his head. If he could get out of this room, it would probably get him shot, but that would be far better than dying with a rope around his neck. If he got out, he might find one chance in a million outside; in here there was no chance at all.

It depended on whether or not the Mountie was alone when he brought them something to eat. He might be able to handle one man—with Daggett's help. But that door was as far as he could plan. What happened outside would have to be improvised.

"Daggett, we might be able to get out of this room."

Daggett's grunt showed little interest, and Brent resisted the impulse to walk over and smash him in the face. "Don't you want to get out of here?"

"What good will it do?" Daggett's tone said that he had quit. "If we do get out of this room, we'll only be shot."

"Would you rather be hanged? I'll take a bullet any damned time."

"How can we get out of here?" Daggett's voice wasn't filled with hope, but it had lifted a little.

"That Mountie said he'd bring us back something to eat. If he comes alone, we might be able to handle him. I'll stand to one side of the door while you take it from him."

"What then?" That was more lift in Daggett's voice.

"It depends on how things work out." Daggett would have to draw what encouragement he could from those unpromising words.

Daggett gave a grudging consent. "I guess we got nothing to lose."

An hour dragged by, and new fury was driving Brent wild. Daggett put it into words. "The bastard's ain't even going to feed us."

Brent heard the noise of the key at the lock and hissed at Daggett. He moved catlike to the door, being sure not to pick the side where the door would swing against him. He reached out and pushed Daggett back a couple of feet. He had to pull the trooper into the room where he could get a chance at him.

The door swung open, and the Mountie stepped inside. He carried a pail of some kind in one hand, a gun in the other. "Here's your—"

The words died in a garbled squawk as Brent seized him from behind. A hard forearm slammed across the man's throat.

Brent startled at how easy it went, almost too easy. The resistance flowed quickly out of the man, and he eased him to the floor. He picked up the dropped pistol and stooped to check his breathing. His mind still picked at the lack of resistance; he had expected far more.

The breathing was shallow and labored. The man was unconscious. He had to keep Daggett from bolting out of the door.

He eased outside, Daggett pushing up against him, and saw no one in the compound. That struck another false note. Macleod was damned careless, or else he thought it was unnecessary to keep a tighter watch. He kept stewing about it, for none of this fitted Macleod's nature as he knew it.

Daggett shoved at him, and Brent snarled. He had to hold Daggett down. Hasty movement would call attention to them quicker than a shout.

He moved along the wall of the buildings, Daggett treading on his heels. A light burned in the room Hampton had used as an office, and two saddled horses were before it.

Brent scowled at them, and some kind of a warning gnawed at him. This was too easy. He almost felt as though those horses were left there to pull him into something. Then another thought struck him. A couple of troopers might have been out on patrol and were reporting to somebody in that room. He didn't know what kind of a chance was being handed him, but he couldn't stand here quarreling with it. He faced the hard, simple fact of taking what was offered to him or nothing.

He moved like a shadow toward the horses, his eyes trying to cover all of the post at once. He stopped Daggett from mounting, knowing the man would have immediately kicked the horse into wild flight. But where would he ride? They still had a gate to get through.

They led the horses across the compound, and Brent felt as though a thousand pairs of eyes watched every step he took. He couldn't believe it, but there was nobody on the gate. He would never have taken Macleod for a lax man. He shook his head. Here he was, quarreling with his luck again.

He thrust his reins into Daggett's hand. "I'll open it."

The gate swung heavily, and its creaking seemed loud enough to be heard for twenty miles. He gave it a final shove, and a horse streaked by, brushing him almost hard enough to knock him down. He cursed Daggett as he ran for the remaining horse. If that squeaking gate hadn't alerted anybody, those pounding hoofs would.

He didn't know where those men came from, but they were all around him. They swarmed him under, smothering his struggles by sheer mass of weight.

He wanted to scream against the inequity of it. Daggett was free, and they had taken him again. He couldn't make a sound; his mouth was full of dust.

21

HE WAS dragged into the lighted room, and Macleod and Moore sat side by side behind a table. Macleod had a tight little smile, and Moore's grin was like the full moon.

"Looks like he put up a pretty good fight," Moore observed.

140

The men holding Brent released him and adjusted their disheveled uniforms. "Pretty good, sir," one of them said.

"Did Daggett get away?" Macleod asked.

"Clean away, sir."

Brent's head whirled, and he couldn't pick a coherent word out of the jumbled mass in his mind.

Another Mountie came into the room, and Macleod asked, "Are you all right, Beatty?"

Beatty nodded. "He's pretty strong, sir. I dropped the minute he took hold of me."

Little bits were falling into place, making a picture for Brent. He was beginning to understand why there had been so many sour notes in that escape. They had staged it all, and they seemed pleased with the outcome.

His rage boiled over, and he swore at Macleod and Moore.

Moore grinned at Macleod. "He seems unhappy, Major. Maybe you better put him back and hang him in the morning."

"He's been through a bad time," Macleod said dryly. "I guess he's earned giving us a little abuse."

The knowledge that he was all right took some time to filter into Brent's head. His swearing ran down and stopped. "Why did you let Daggett go?"

Moore's face sobered. "I still want the man who built Whoop-up. I'm hoping Daggett will lead me to him. He's broke and scared. I think he'll head straight back to Benton."

"How did you know where I was?"

"Daggett sent Molly a letter by one of the freighters. He promised her big things, and she talked about it. She's another reason he'll go back to Benton." He turned his head to Macleod. "Major, do you remember the first one you turned lose? A Bob Beary?" At Macleod's nod, he continued. "He got back to Benton, and you should've heard some of the merchants who backed the independent traders scream. They talked about taking an army into Canada and recovering their property. They got that idea out of their heads in a hurry after I talked to them. They were pretty happy to shut up and forget the whole thing in a hurry. I'm afraid the man

I want knows all about it. I'll never dig him out unless Daggett leads me to him."

Remnants of rage still simmered in Brent. He glared at Macleod. "You took a hell of a chance. I might've killed one of your men."

Macleod nodded. "I considered all of the risks. I want to see the man who built Whoop-up brought to justice as badly as Moore does. He got here just as I was preparing to ride against the fort. We worked it out together, and I decided it worth the risks."

Brent was still outraged. "If he hadn't gotten here when he did, I would've been hanged."

Macleod's face was calm under the shouted accusation. "No. It wasn't a hanging offense. You would have gotten the same sentence as the others."

It kicked all the props from under Brent's anger; it left him feeling awkward and foolish. His belly rumbled, and he growled, "You might at least feed me."

Macleod laughed. "We've got a meal waiting for you."

Moore sat with Brent while he ate. "You did a job, Brent. I'm proud of you."

"I didn't learn the name of the man you wanted."

"He's not lost."

Brent began eating faster. Daggett was putting miles between himself and the fort. "We'd better be getting after Daggett."

"You're not going. It's a long way between here and the border. I'll pick him up before he gets out of Canada."

Brent laid down his fork. "What am I supposed to be doing?"

"Stay here with Macleod for a little while. All of the tribes are coming in in a week or ten days to sign a treaty. I want you to see it."

Brent had had a bellyful of looking at Indians. "Damn it, Lucas—"

"Stay, Brent." Moore made it a request instead of an order. "I think it will be worthwhile to you."

Brent sighed. He wanted to refuse him, but he didn't. It didn't seem as though he could get away from this place.

Macleod was tense with excitement the morning of the

treaty signing. All day yesterday the tribes had been arriving, and the lodges stood in solid rows before the fort.

Macleod gazed out over them. "Bloods, Piegans, Blackfeet, Crees, and Assiniboines. For the first time in I don't know how many years, living in peace, side by side. Even if it's only for a few days, it's a start." His eyes had a shine to them. "This treaty could mean peace for a hundred years or more. Do you know what makes them feel as though they can trust us? Smashing the whiskey traders."

Brent's face was dubious. "Do you really think they're smashed?"

Macleod nodded. "In the main, yes. A few of them will try again. The profits will lure them. But we'll knock it out of their heads in a hurry."

His eyes went back to the lodges. "This afternoon will be a time of ceremony. Speech after speech. But I think you will find them interesting. I'll see that you have interpreters. The chiefs will be escorted to the council, and their people will watch. You know," he said thoughtfully, "these people have a great dignity. If only we'd take the time to understand it." He moved away to attend to another of the hundred details that pressed him.

Brent didn't believe he could become this interested. He had seen the Indian at his worst; now he saw him at his best. It made a difference, he admitted.

Button Chief, a minor leader of the Bloods, spoke first, and an intrepeter translated for Brent. "The Great Spirit sent the white man across the great waters to carry out His ends. The Great Spirit, and not the Great Mother, gave us this land. But the Great Mother sent Stamixotokon and the police to put an end to the traffic in firewater."

The interpreter said swiftly, "Stamixotokon, meaning buffalo bull's head, from the uniform insignia bearing the police crest."

Brent nodded. He was absorbed in Button Chief's words.

"Now I can sleep safely," Button Chief went on. "Before the arrival of the police, when I laid my head down at night, every sound frightened me; my sleep was broken; now I can sleep sound, and I am not afraid. The police have proved themselves. I say that in the future all matters of trouble should be handled by them."

He looked around proudly before he sat down.

"Eagle Tail, head chief of the North Piegans," another interpreter said to Brent.

Eagle Tail had the same simple dignity as he looked at the assembled chieftains and treaty commissioners. "When the police first came to this country, I met and shook hands with Stamixotokon. Since that time he has made me many promises. He kept them all. Not one of them was ever broken. Everything that the police have done has been good. I trust Stamixotokon and will leave everything to him."

Crowfoot, head chief of the South Blackfeet and the immortal statesman of his tribe, followed. "The advice given me and my people has proved to be very good. If the police had not come to this country, where would we all be by now? Bad men and whiskey were killing us so fast that very few indeed would have been left by the next year. The police have protected us as the feathers of the bird protect it from the frosts of winter. I wish them all good and trust that all our hearts will increase in goodness from this time forward. I am satisfied. I will sign the treaty."

The speeches went on and on, but Brent found not a single one of them boring. A growing pride swelled in him for these people. My people, he thought, and for the first time he didn't shrink from the blood he had always hated.

There was more ceremony as signatures were affixed to the treaty papers and payments distributed.

Macleod, or Stamixotokon, was the last speaker. "The treaty promises will be kept. If they were broken, I would be ashamed to look you in the face. But every promise will be solemnly fulfilled as certainly as the sun now shines down upon us from the heavens."

He stopped and thrust out his hands to the chiefs. Their granite faces softened, and they smiled at their friend. "I shall always remember," Macleod said, "the kind manner in which you have spoken of me."

The chiefs and Macleod ceremoniously shook hands. He stood rigidly at attention and watched them stalk grandly out of the council enclosure and across the field to their tribes.

Brent recalled what one of the chiefs had said. "Before the police came, the Indian walked bent; now he walks erect."

And so all of them walked, proudly erect, proudly bearing presents which were pledges of the Great White Mother's good faith: the treaty flags, the silver medals, and—most of all—the red coats.

One man had accomplished all this; Macleod had given them their dignity back. It suddenly occurred to Brent that Moore was cast in the same mold as Macleod; he had worked as hard and as dedicatedly. But he wouldn't know the satisfaction Macleod must know today. I hope he finds the man he wants, Brent thought.

Macleod came over to him, and there was a question in his eyes. "I'll never forget this, Major."

The question left Macleod's eyes; he was satisfied. "You'll be riding back to Fort Benton?"

"As soon as I can leave."

"I thought you would. Your horse is saddled."

A trooper led Brent's horse to him. He swung into the saddle and looked at Macleod.

Macleod reached up his hand. "I hate to see you go. I hope we'll meet again someday."

Brent took the firm grip of that hand, and a grin spread over his face. "But not in a courtroom, Major."

Macleod's laughter rang in his ears as he rode out of the gate.

22

THE WAITING had scraped Daggett's nerves raw. Wasn't that goddamned Nader ever coming back to town? Daggett no longer felt any threat of danger to him, for he was on familiar and safe ground, but that had been close in Whoop-up. Occasionally he wondered if Brent had gotten out. He had looked back a dozen times, but he had never seen him. He made no other effort to find out about Brent. He had his own skin to look after.

Being broke was the greatest grind. He hadn't had any money in the past half week. Last night he and Molly had had one hell of a fight. She had screeched at him and ordered him out. But she didn't mean that "never come back." He knew how fast she would change her mind if he could show her a little money. He slammed the heel of his palm against the rail of a hitching rack, and a passerby looked curiously at him. Daggett's eyes turned ugly, inviting the man to comment. But the man ducked his head and hurried on by. That damned Nader would pick this time to make a trip to St. Louis. His office had expected him before now, but he wasn't back yet. Daggett would give him a few more days at the most. Nader's whiskey-trading business was gone, but he wouldn't want Fort Benton and Lucas Moore, particularly, knowing about it. Nader would pay a good sum to keep that quiet.

Daggett stopped walking as a new phase of the idea hit him. How valuable was the name of Nader to Moore? That might be worth investigating. A man was always better off if he had two strings to his bow.

He resumed his slow walk. Mr. Nader was going to get four more days and no more. It was the first time he had set a definite time limit. When four days were gone, he would see Moore. One way or another he was going to get some money to put into his pocket.

He passed the place where Molly worked and stared longingly over the swinging doors. He made no attempt to enter. After last night he knew better.

Brent found Moore in the hotel lobby. He had heard the mournful whistling of a steamboat as he had ridden into Benton. Leaving or coming in? He didn't know. Those pilots and captains loved to yank on that whistle cord. He found no comfort in being back in town. This place no longer had any attractions for him.

Moore was seated in a chair with his back to the door. His clasped hands hung below his knees, and he stared broodingly at the toes of his boots.

"Is this what you get paid for?"

"Brent!" Moore's cry pulled every head in the lobby toward them. The brooding was swept from his face. He wrung Brent's hand until Brent thought he was going to twist the arm out of its socket. "My God, I'm glad to see you, Brent."

"Lucas, I stayed until it was over."

Moore's searching look was reminiscent of the way Macleod had looked after the treaty signing. "What did you think about it?"

"I think the white man hasn't given them too much of a chance."

Moore's eyes were grave, and Brent smiled. "That's what you wanted me to see, wasn't it?"

"Yes." It was a simple word, but it expressed everything.

Too many people were trying to hear what they were saying, and Moore pulled him over to a secluded corner. "That Macleod is quite a man."

Brent couldn't disagree with that. But Macleod had everything in his favor. He thought Moore looked sort of wistful. "Lucas, he's got different conditions than you have. They gave him all the men he needed. He's his own court and prosecutor. He also makes his own verdicts and sentences without some politician meddling in them and changing them. It makes a difference."

Moore's smile was feeble as he nodded. "I guess it does. But he still cleaned up the job I wanted to do. It was our thunder mug, Brent. We were the ones who should have emptied it."

The heaviness of his words gave Brent his first inkling that Moore had had no success at all. "You lost Daggett?"

"I followed him all the way to Benton."

Brent frowned. "He didn't see anybody?"

"The ordinary run. Nobody that I couldn't check out."

"You had to miss somewhere. Why else would he come back?"

Moore sighed. "I don't know. He's broke. Molly threw him out last night because of it. But he hasn't contacted anybody big enough to have the money to back Whoop-up."

The frown remained on Brent's face. "Lucas, that man has to be here."

"I've watched Daggett twelve hours a day. My deputy watched him the other twelve. We put him to bed at night and got him up in the morning. You tell me where we've missed."

Brent couldn't see it, but it had to be there. Any other reason for Daggett coming back here didn't make sense. He knew Daggett left Whoop-up with little or no money. Where would he get a new supply, except from the man who had hired him?

Moore sighed. "I sure wish you'd heard him say who he was working for."

Brent had been wishing that for weeks. That would have made it easy for both of them. He shook his head.

Moore had a half-hopeful expression on his face. "Are you sure you didn't hear a name that you forgot?"

Brent's face was indignant. He had been sent to Whoop-up to learn a name. If he had heard it, would he be careless enough to forget it?

"I overheard every conversation I could. There weren't too many. Hampton and Daggett had bad feeling between them. They didn't talk to each other much. The rest of the men there didn't know anything. Or if they did, I couldn't get it out of them. The only thing I heard up there was Hampton and Daggett talking about neighbors."

Moore's eyes widened. "Neighbors? Up there?"

"They were talking about Macleod after he moved into the country."

Moore's voice was low pitched as he hit the heel of his palm against his knee. "Maybe it's been there right in front of my eyes all the time, and I've been too blind to see it. Hell, it all fits, and I never even thought of him."

Brent didn't have the slightest idea of what Moore was talking about. "I'm glad you think you see something," he grumbled.

"Could it have been Nader instead of neighbors?" Moore was tense as he waited for Brent's answer.

"I don't know, Lucas." Moore could be reaching into thin air, trying to grab a handful of nothing.

"It fits, Brent. Nader's big enough to finance it."

Brent hated to flatten Moore's new hope, but he had to do it. "Then why hasn't Daggett tried to see him?"

Moore's excitement was getting more visible by the moment. "Because Nader's been out of town. His office expects him back any day now."

Brent remembered the boat whistle he had heard. Some of Moore's excitement spilled over onto him.

"Daggett's been at the bank several times, Brent. He

always came right back out. I thought he was drawing money or maybe trying to make a loan. How stupid can a man be? He's been waiting for Nader to return."

Brent's pulses were hammering now, perhaps as hard as Moore's. His grin was unsteady as he stood. "We'd better go see if you're right. Or just guessing. First, I guess we better find out if Nader came back tonight."

A man came into the lobby, and his eyes swept it. He saw Moore and started toward him.

"Long, my deputy," Moore said. "By the looks of his face, he's unhappy about something."

He introduced Long to Brent. "The one I told you about who was up at Whoop-up."

Long was a sandy-haired man with a thin, naturally unhappy face. The unhappiness was increased by some inner self-accusation.

"Lucas, I lost him. One minute Daggett was standing right in front of my eyes. I spoke to a friend. I swear I hardly took my eyes off of Daggett. But when I looked around, he was gone."

Brent remembered the night he had lost Daggett in much the same manner. And he remembered how tough it had been to report it to Moore. "Were you near the alley across from Smithson's store?"

Long nodded. A flush started in his face at Brent's grin, and his chin jutted belligerently. "What's so goddamned funny about it?"

Brent flicked his eyes to Moore. "Lucas, does that alley run behind Nader's bank?"

Moore drew a deep breath. "It sure as hell does. Don't worry about it, Long. Maybe we know where Daggett is."

"Will somebody tell me what this is all about?" Long yelped.

"We're not sure we know, ourselves, Long. We'll explain it later. You take a place in front of Nader's bank. Arrest anybody that comes out. Shoot them if they resist. The back door belongs to us, doesn't it, Brent?"

Brent nodded soberly. "I think it does, Lucas."

They moved soundlessly down the dark alley, each man wrapped in his own thoughts. This had to be it, Brent thought. Moore would be sick if it all turned out to be unfounded guesses. Just the thought of it all being empty guesses made him feel a little sick right now.

The back of Nader's bank was dark. Brent's heart sank. He didn't know exactly what he had expected, but not this black silence.

Moore saw it first. The blind had been drawn, but a crack of light showed along one side of the window. Brent's heart came up. Somebody was in there.

They moved to the rear door and put their ears close to it. They could hear the murmur of voices, but not a clear word carried to them. Then a voice was raised in vicious anger. "Why, you bastard. You've got the nerve to come here and threaten me?"

Moore nodded to Brent, and both drew guns. "Daggett," Brent whispered. Daggett belonged to him, and Moore nodded his understanding. He pulled Brent back a half step and raised his foot.

The boot crashed into the door handle, and it shuddered and split before it flew open. Maybe it hadn't been locked, but Moore couldn't take the chance of finding out and alerting whoever was inside.

He was through the door before it banged against the wall, and Brent was right on his heels. He stepped quickly to one side, and Nader and Daggett were held in some kind of a shock, their mouths sagging open. The lamplight picked up the growing whiteness in their faces.

"You're under arrest, Nader," Moore said. "Both of you."

Nader flashed an insane glance at Daggett. "You son-of-a-bitch. You led them to me."

He looked back at Moore, and his eyes weighed many things: the loss of everything he had, the disgrace, the jail term. He had no chance at all against Moore's drawn gun, but perhaps he decided it was better than the other that faced him.

Moore saw his final decision and yelled, "Don't do it, Nader."

Brent kept his eyes on Daggett. The man was just throwing off the initial shock. Moore's warning and the drawn pistols weren't going to be enough to stop either of them.

It was suicidal, but they tried. Brent waited until Daggett's hand closed on the pistol butt. He shot him in the stomach before the gun cleared its holster. He heard a hammering report beside him and was vaguely aware of Nader stumbling backward. Daggett went high on his toes, his arms wrapping around his wound. He seemed to hang there indefinitely before he plunged forward on his face. He looked desperately up at Brent, and a sudden rush of blood blocked whatever he wanted to say. He made a sudden convulsive movement and rolled over on his side.

Moore was shaking his head as he put away his gun. "The damned fools. But maybe this choice was better than the one that faced them."

He walked forward and bent over Nader. "Dead." His eyes were bleak.

Brent rolled Daggett over on his back. "This one isn't. But he's hit hard."

Moore's face brightened. "I'll get the Doc. I'd sure like to have him talk."

Brent shook his head. Moore was going to be disappointed again. He was suddenly very tired.

23

MOORE HAILED Brent just as he came out of the hotel in the morning. Brent turned indifferently. The night's sleep had done nothing to erase his weariness.

Moore caught up with him. "Daggett died this morning." His voice had a hard satisfaction. "He talked before he did. Nader wasn't going to give him anything. I think Daggett died happy, knowing Nader was dead. A couple of witnesses heard him tell all about Whoop-up."

Brent understood his satisfaction. Moore didn't have to explain to some authority that his killing Nader was based only on conjecture.

"I guess it's over, Lucas."

"This part of it is. A few others will still try it. It's going to be hard for them to let go of all those profits."

That was odd. He used much the same words as Macleod had.

"Brent, what are you going to do now?"

Brent shook his head. He hadn't the slightest idea and cared less. Drift on someplace, he supposed, until something caught his fancy.

"I can offer you a permanent job."

Brent didn't even consider it. He didn't regret the past months, but he wanted no more of it. He was partially lying to himslf. He did regret about Paula. He wished he had never known her. How long did it take for a man to get a girl out of his head?

"Brent, consider it."

Brent shook his head again and started to turn away

"Brent, Brent."

He knew that voice, and he didn't want to turn in its direction. He made his face wooden before he faced her.

She ran across the street to him, and her eyes were blazing. She ignored Moore completely. "Why did you leave?"

He let a shrug answer for him. That hurt her; he saw it in her eyes.

"You didn't even have enough manners to say goodbye."

He winced inwardly; that stung. So Dawes hadn't said a thing to her. He had just let her wonder and ache. He wasn't going to take that from Dawes, and anger broke up the woodenness in his face.

"Your father kicked me off. Because of my Indian blood. Paula, he would've shot me if I hadn't left."

Her anger was in full flame, and for a moment he thought it was directed at him. The Indian blood again, he knew with miserable certainty.

"Why damn him," she raved. "I'm an eighth Choctaw. Grandmother's a full half. If he wanted Mother, he took Grandmother." Her breast heaved in agitation. "He's been ashamed of me all this time."

Brent was sorry he was the cause of her unhappiness, but she was wrong. Anybody could see how Church Dawes felt about her. "No, Paula. You're wrong."

"Damn him, damn him, damn him," she raved. "I'll show him." A sudden decision firmed in her face. "Brent, come back with me. If he doesn't accept you, I'll leave with you Anyplace you want to go. Brent, I'm begging you."

"I wouldn't let a girl like her beg me," Moore drawled.

Brent flashed him an angry glance. "Stay out of this." He was wracked by indecision. He didn't have the right to take her away. What did he have to offer her?

Her eyes searched his face, and her eyes went dead as she crumpled from within.

"I thought he was tough enough to face anything," Moore said. "He isn't. Not when it comes to Church Dawes."

Brent swore at him. "I told you to stay out of this."

"Somebody has to do your thinking for you. Somebody has to put a little backbone in you. What's Church Dawes? Another man. She isn't afraid of him. But then, she's a better man than you are."

Brent drew back his fist. Another word was going to earn Moore a smash in the mouth. He looked at two pair of eyes, withholding their judgment as they waited. These two people meant more to him than all the rest of the world.

He drew a deep breath, trying to smother the last of the uneasiness. It was a stubborn thing; a spark of it remained.

He took hold of her arm. "Let's go, Paula." His voice was almost steady.

The light came back into her eyes, and she pressed tight against him. He heard a catch in her voice and was sure she was going to cry.

Moore stood there with a big grin, and people watched all along the street. Brent didn't want anybody seeing her break down. He pushed her away to arm's length. "Easy."

A blaze was in her eyes; she hadn't been ready to break down at all. But the blaze wasn't directed at him. "You wait until I say a few things to him."

"I'll do the talking," he said crisply. If she was going to leave Dawes, he wanted to keep the bad feelings to a minimum.

Rebellion sparked in her eyes, then she said meekly, "Yes, Brent."

"I think I'll ride along with you," Moore observed.

Brent started to yell at him, then held it. Maybe it would be best if Moore was along. This was going to hit Dawes hard, and nobody could tell what that wild man would do. Moore's presence might put a halter on him. Brent admitted it. He was scared of Church Dawes.

He smiled at her. "Ready?"

Her eyes held so many things for him, most of all a shining pride. How could a man worry about the future when he looked into eyes like that?

Dawes saw them coming and stood rigidly awaiting them. A half-dozen of his riders were with him, Sandy among them.

Brent was hollow inside. But anybody with any sense would get that hollowness if he had to look at that thundercloud face.

Dawes didn't say a word until they dismounted. Then he strode forward and seized Paula's wrist. "Get away from that damned Indian."

She jerked her wrist free, and hot words trembled on her lips. Then she remembered her promise to Brent and held them.

She had a long ruler to measure him by, and if his voice trembled, he would cut his throat. "She's coming away with me." He almost said, Mr. Dawes, and caught it in time. He made it Church instead.

Dawes tried to force too many words out at once, and they jammed up inside his mouth. When they finally came, they shook the surrounding hills. "Why, you goddamned Indian. Get on that horse and ride, or there won't be enough left of you to feed the dogs."

"I'll throw him off for you, boss," Sandy said eagerly.

Brent flashed him a fierce glance. That was something else that was going to have to be taken care of.

Paula could hold her words no longer. "I'm leaving with him. I'm not ashamed of my Indian blood. But you are."

Dawes looked stricken, and his groan sounded as though it came from mortal hurt. "Aw, Paula, you know better than that."

She remorselessly flayed him. "And you were ashamed of Mother, too. All this time you've been ashamed of us."

Dawes' face stiffened. "That's a damned lie, and you know it. When I lost her, I thought I was going to die."

She had absolutely no mercy for him. "You show it."

154

Brent pushed her back. She didn't have to talk for him. "You lost some stock to Indians, and you hate all Indian blood. You're blaming them instead of yourself. You took their land and drove their game away. What did you expect them to do? Starve?"

Dawes' nostrils pinched tight under his heavy breathing. "Now just a goddamned minute."

"Shut up," Brent roared. "I was ashamed of my Indian blood, too. But I've seen Indians that make the white man look like wolves. I saw more dignity, more honor, among them than I ever found in a lot of white men. I've been ashamed of the wrong blood all the time." He took Paula's arm. "Come on, Paula."

"I've got to get Grandmother, Brent."

He nodded full approval.

Dawes' face fell into ruin. "No, Paula," he groaned. "Don't kill me all over again."

Her eyes were sort of crinkled, but her face was as resolute as ever. "I go where he goes."

Dawes' sigh tore out his heart and offered it to her. "If he stays right here, Paula? I'll give him a job, a lifetime job."

The crinkling around her eyes was more pronounced. "It's up to Brent."

Brent thought he should finish clubbing Dawes to the ground. He looked at her, and his face softened. "The first time you yell at me . . ." He let the threat die. Dawes would yell often in the future; it was his nature. But maybe a mutual respect would build slowly.

Dawes wouldn't meet his eyes, but he stuck out his hand. "It'll work out," he muttered.

Sandy said in a too-loud voice. "Now we've got that damned Indian around here all the time."

Brent whirled on him. "And that's something we're going to talk over."

His intentions were plain in every line of him. "Brent," Paula cried.

He put those fierce eyes on her. He didn't have to tell her to stay out of it.

Sandy's eyes were aflame with eagerness. "When I get through with you, you'll be glad to run."

Brent hit him right in the middle of that big mouth. It was

a good solid blow; it had muscle and all of the past abuse behind it.

Sandy's feet flipped up into the air, and he went down with a bone-cracking thump. He lay there, a dazed expression on his face, his eyes vague and watery.

Brent stood over him, waiting for his eyes to focus. He had to admit Sandy was tough. That blow should have put him out. "Get up. Or are you all mouth?"

Sandy's eyes cleared. He climbed unsteadily back on his feet. "Ah." The word carried some kind of satisfaction.

Brent was too anxious, and Sandy slipped the blow over his shoulder. The next thing Brent knew, he was on his back, looking up at Sandy. His head rang, and his chin was the focal point of a spreading numbness.

"Your legs ain't very strong, Indian. One little piddling punch and down you go."

Brent saw different emotions on different faces. Dawes looked happy; Paula was distressed; Moore wore his worry openly. But worst of all, Sandy was jeering. That pulled him back to his feet. He didn't intend to make any more eager mistakes.

Maybe Sandy's blow wasn't all mistake, he thought after an exchange of a half-dozen blows. Sandy was strong, and he hit with authority. Brent dripped blood from a split lip, and Sandy had a cut under his eye. Both men panted as they moved. Brent noticed the jeering remarks had stopped.

He dug a fist into Sandy's belly and caught the jaw as Sandy doubled over. He knocked him down again, and Sandy looked at him a long time with speculative eyes. But he was getting up again. What did it take to keep the man down?

He was the stronger now, and he knew it. Now it was just a matter of standing off and whittling on Sandy until he couldn't get up.

How in the hell did he find himself on the ground again? Somebody beat a big drum in his head. He saw three Sandys, all of them swirling around him. None of the three Sandys were jeering; in fact, they all looked pretty grim.

Brent waited until the three figures merged into one. He didn't want to get up, but he had to. He couldn't stop with Paula and Dawes watching.

Something had taken the bones out of his legs, and the legs

insisted on bending on him. He wobbled toward Sandy, knowing he couldn't possibly look as bad as he felt. He went straight in, and he thought he heard a splattering noise. That must have come from his face, for his head rocked back. But that was all, and he thought in surprise, He can't hurt me.

He threw away all subtlety. Something kept peppering away against his face and body, and whatever it was couldn't keep him from reaching Sandy. He clubbed him on the ear, and as Sandy's head turned under the blow, he aimed for the jaw. He went in too high, landing on the cheekbone, and Sandy reeled backards and fell.

Brent made pawing motions with his hands. "Come on. Get up."

It took Sandy a long time. He made it to a knee, and the leg buckled under him, dumping him. He had to begin it all over, and it was a slow and painful procedure.

Brent watched that struggle. He hoped Sandy didn't make it. A lot of man was trying to get back on his feet. Brent didn't want to hit him again.

Sandy made it and stood weaving. One good eye searched for Brent. The other was closed. "Where are you, Indian?" Each word sprayed bloody specks.

The name spurred Brent again. He had a clear target to the chin, and he landed fair. Sandy wouldn't get up from that one.

He stared in disbelief. Sandy was trying. He got his hands under him and braced his arms enough to raise his face and torso from the ground. Brent suddenly felt every throbbing hurt. They swirled around him, screaming in fiendish voices. And his arms had great weights fastened to the ends of them. He would never be able to lift them again.

Sandy's arms broke and dropped his face into the dust again. It was impossible, but he was raising his head. He glared at Brent with that one undaunted eye. "Don't just stand there. Help me up."

It was no time to be laughing, but the sound gurgled in Brent's throat. He reached down and took the hand lifted to him. He thought Sandy was going to pull him over, but he managed to haul the man to his feet. Sandy's knees went first one way, then the other, and Brent put an arm around him in support.

They staggered toward the horse trough, and none of the watchers were unwise enough to offer help. They went down on their knees beside the trough, and Brent splashed water into his face. If he thought the hurts howled at him before, he was wrong. The water really gave them voice.

Sandy stopped his splashing and looked at him with a new appraisal. "You know, Indian, you're pretty tough."

Brent stretched out his hand and pushed Sandy's head under. It didn't take much of a shove, just laying his hand on Sandy's head was enough. And there wasn't the slightest malice in the shoving.

Sandy came up blowing, and the water dripped pink from his chin.

Paula rushed toward them. "Brent," she wailed, "look at your face."

Sandy leered at her. "I think it looks right pretty."

She turned on him, all teeth and claws. "Sandy, I'll kill you for this."

"Paula, get away from here." Brent tried to roar, and at that, it was a fair effort.

She looked at him uncertainly, then turned and fled.

Sandy watched her with a speculative gleam, then he put that gleam on Brent. "You know, if I had to pick a fair man, I guess I'd have to pick you."

Brent had his own confession to make. "I couldn't let myself get whipped with her watching me."

Sandy tried a grin that turned into a grimace. "I'll keep that in mind when I figure you next time. If I ever get the memory of this one out of my head."

Paula stood with Dawes' arm about her shoulders. "Look at them, grinning at each other like idiots," she said furiously. "What did they prove?"

"They settled something in their own minds, Paula," Moore said gently. He grinned at Dawes. "I'd say you picked yourself a good man for a son-in-law."

Dawes snorted. His face was frosty, but he couldn't hide the shine in his eyes.

"Sandy accepted him," Moore prodded.

Dawes' snort was louder. "That's his way. People have to accept him. He just forces himself on them."

That familiar flare was appearing in Paula's face, and

158

Moore shook his head at her. The flare faded, and a tremulous smile replaced it.

"What are you two laughing at?" Dawes demanded. He couldn't control the quirking at the corners of his mouth. It grew and grew, and three smiles turned toward the two men at the horse trough.

Wade Everett, a pseudonym for Will Cook, is the author of numerous outstanding Western novels as well as historical frontier fiction. He was born in Richmond, Indiana, but was raised by an aunt and uncle in Cambridge, Illinois. He joined the U.S. cavalry at the age of sixteen but was disillusioned because horses were being eliminated through mechanization. He transferred to the U.S. Army Air Force in which he served in the South Pacific during the Second World War. Cook turned to writing in 1951 and contributed a number of outstanding short stories to *Dime Western* and other pulp magazines as well as fiction for major smooth-paper magazines such as *The Saturday Evening Post*. It was in the *Post* that his best-known novel, *Comanche Captives*, was serialized. It was later filmed as *Two Rode Together* (Columbia, 1961) directed by John Ford and starring James Stewart and Richard Widmark. It has now been restored, as was the author's intention, with *The Peacemakers* set in 1870 as the first part and *Comanche Captives* set in 1874 as the second part of a major historical novel titled *Two Rode Together*. Sometimes in his short stories Cook would introduce characters that would later be featured in novels, such as Charlie Boomhauer who first appeared in *Lawmen Die Sudden* in *Big-Book Western* in 1953 and is later to be found in *Badman's Holiday* (1958) and *The Wind River Kid* (1958). Along with his steady productivity, Cook maintained an enviable quality. His novels range widely in time and place, from the Illinois frontier of 1811 to southwest Texas in 1905, but each is peopled with credible and interesting characters whose interactions form the backbone of the narrative. Most of his novels deal with more or less traditional Western themes—range wars, reformed outlaws, cattle rustling, Indian fighting—but there are also romantic novels such as *Sabrina Kane* (1956) and exercises in historical realism such as *Elizabeth, by Name* (1958). Indeed, his fiction is known for its strong heroines. Another common feature is Cook's compassion for his characters who must be able to survive in a wild and violent land. His protagonists make mistakes, hurt people they care for, and sometimes succumb to ignoble impulses, but this all provides an added dimension to the artistry of his work.